Magic

Diamondsong

A Concerto in Ten Parts

Part 04:
Magic

E.D.E. Bell

Atthis Arts
Detroit, Michigan

Diamondsong
Part 04: Magic

Copyright ©2019 by E.D.E. Bell
edebell.com

This is a work of fiction.
Any resemblance to actual pyrsi, winged or otherwise, is purely coincidental.

Cover Art by M.C. Krauss

Map of Ada-ji by Ulla Thynell

Interior Design by G.C. Bell

Editorial Services by:
Camille Gooderham Campbell
Catherine Jones Payne and Haley Tomaszewski, Quill Pen Editorial
M. Cusack

All rights reserved.

Published by Atthis Arts, LLC
Detroit, Michigan
atthisarts.com

ISBN 978-1-945009-38-9

Library of Congress Control Number: 2019935921

First Edition: Published April 2019

This book is dedicated to the magicians of 8235.

Especially Dr. R. L. Bostick
for supporting me
from that time
I held my first signing
during a blizzard
in Bellbrook.

Preface

Most of all, I really just want to thank you for joining me on this journey. I know this serial is experimental, and now that we're solidly into it, I'm both nervous and excited about carrying it out into something meaningful, and something people will enjoy reading.

I especially want to thank Catherine Jones Payne; her insights on this part were extraordinarily helpful, and really, caused me to do a complete and total rewrite of almost every scene.

This part is coming out, admittedly, at a time when I have loaded a bit too much onto my plate. Atthis Arts has several big releases this spring, I've had some personal and professional setbacks, and I've been spending a lot of nights at the Hotel Stormcove. So more than ever, I want to thank the team for getting me through this. Camille Gooderham Campbell, Meghan Cusack, Sasha Kasoff Moore, Laura Johnson, Deborah Reilly, and Maria Judge—you're my magic.

Let's see . . . Dime has just learned something important, and she's staying at that sur IC den with the unattractive wallpaper. We should go check in on her.

To Ada-ji.

Cheers,

E.D.E. Bell

April 2019

THE WORLD OF ADA-JI

The Ja-lal: A humanoid species, dwelling in the foothills and plains of Ada-ji, characterized by broad advancements in construction, invention, and health. The Fo-ror call them brutes.

The Fo-ror: A winged humanoid species, dwelling in the forests of Ada-ji, characterized by their natural living and the use of magical powers, known as valence. The Ja-lal call them fairies.

The Ja-lal and Fo-ror are similar in form, with gray skin, but differences between them in composition and culture. Pyr is singular for a Ja-lal or Fo-ror and pyrsi is plural.

The pyrsi of Ada-ji hold many **gender identities**. While this doesn't clarify all aspects of gender, it is polite to introduce oneself with a prefix, indicating the appropriate pronouns:

Fe' indicates a set of feminine identities, using the pronouns she/her/her(s).

Ma' indicates a set of masculine identities, using the pronouns he/him/his.

Ji' indicates a set of spectrum identities, using the pronouns ve/ver/vis.

When gender is unknown, it is polite to refer to a pyr with xe/xem/xyr(s). Any group of pyrsi (plural) would be referred to with they/them/their(s).

A pyr may be generically referred to as **Burge**, short for the more formal Burgess, often for purposes of polite address or getting a stranger's attention. This is similar to the use of Sir or Ma'am on Earth. For those who hold social prejudice based on class, the term implies some sense of status or honor.

Ja-lal and Fo-ror may live up to 50 cycles. Their lives are divided into defined **epochs**, aligning with societal expectations:

Aoch	Age 0-9	Characterized by upbringing, education, and exploration
Bakh	Age 10-19	Centered on building family, performing and completing apprenticeships, and finalizing life plans
Gamh	Age 20-29	Fully immersed in their specialty or role, contributing full-time to society
Dorh	Age 30-39	Respected in leadership and/or advisory roles; it is normal to take some time for self
Eroh	Age 40+	Expected to retire and engage in craft or occasional consulting, through the **life expectancy of around 50 cycles**.

Expectations differ for each culture. For example, while a Ja-lal must develop xyr profession into a career, a Fo-ror's profession and rank are set based on xyr social class and other historical and cultural factors.

A **cycle** on Ada-ji is perhaps up to four times the length of an Earth year. So, our main character, at age 20.5 cycles, has lived more than 80 Earth years but, in relation to her life span, could be considered at the **maturity of her early forties** on Earth.

Each **turn** on Ada-ji, a period of day and then night, is **significantly longer than an Earth day**. As such, pyrsi do not sleep according to light or dark, but instead based on their own needs, lifestyle, profession, and schedule.

The Ja-lal measure time by the periodic sounding of bells; they refer to the resultant time periods with the same term. The Fo-ror are less rigid about time-keeping and refer to the equivalent time period as a span. Each **bell**, or **span**, consists of more than two Earth hours.

Smaller amounts of time are referred to by both cultures as **takes**, which can be thought of as about ten Earth minutes.

In Earth terms, it has been about five weeks since the beginning of our tale.

The Ja-lal and Fo-ror live on separate sides of the Great Cliff. They have not interacted since the ***Great War***, an event most noted for being the **end of the Violence** on Ada-ji.

Synopsis to Here

Fe'Diamond, known as Dime, had just left her career working for the Circles, the government of the Ja-lal. Suddenly, three hooded figures burst into her home with ropes, demanding to take her away. Without any understanding of why this had occurred, Dime and her spouse, Dayn, ran to escape them.

The intruders were revealed to be Fo-ror, commonly known as fairies. These fairies, unseen since the conclusion of the Great War, were feared and loathed by the Ja-lal, who were taught that any contact would cause the Violence to return. The fairies were said to employ a magical power known as valence, but Dime had thought this a myth—perhaps that even the fairies themselves were a myth—until she saw both herself.

Dime escaped from the city and, finally evading the fairies' continued pursuit, she was rescued by a large animal species known as newts. Living amongst them, she befriended a young newt she called Juni. It became apparent to her that the Fo-ror had driven the newts from their original home, keeping them away from Fo-ror civilization with large barriers of rope netting. She was brought back to Sol's Reach by a fe'pyr familiar with fairies, Ella, who broke the news that, for reasons yet unknown, Dime was biologically a Fo-ror—one whose wings had been removed.

After recovering, Dime traveled to the land of the fairies, the Heartland, to learn more about her past. There, in the city, Pito, she found that her old colleague and former flame, Agent Rock, had gone to find her, landing herself in Fo-ror prison. Rock helped Dime escape, with Dime promising to return to assist Rock.

Dime met with the High Seat, Ferala, who confessed that she was part of an old scheme to avenge the horrors of a disease called the curse, which the Fo-ror blamed on the Ja-lal. This scheme, designed by now Third Seat Neimano, was named Project Diamondsong. His plan was to remove the wings from Fo-ror newborns, place them in positions of potential influence amongst the Ja-lal, and then allow them to grow up before activating their loyalties as Fo-ror spies.

Dime returned to Sol's Reach, where she visited family and friends in secret, and also snuck into the Circles' complex to find clues that would point her to potential other victims of Project Diamondsong. She was only able to locate two others: Kolk and Nafat, both of whom she informed of their history and biology to different results. Just as Dime returned to her family, the Sol's Pillars, a fringe group who believes Dime is working with the fairies, surrounded them, pursuing as they tried to leave the city.

Responding to Dime's earlier call for help, Ella arrived, followed by Juni. Tum, whose wheelchair was broken as they fled, was carried off, with everyone's concurrence, by Juni. Finally, when a pyr threatened Dime's nearly-grown child, Luja, Dime reacted subconsciously, causing a large rift in the rock that allowed them to escape. Dayn, Luja, and Ella made their way to a hiding place far from Lodon, with Dime in a continuing state of shock. There, once Dime had recovered, Ella explained that valence did not come from the wings, it came from the heart. She recommended that Dime travel to the diamond caves to better learn how to use and control her powers.

Dime is preparing, emotionally as well as physically, for the journey back to the Heartland, while Dayn and Luja wait at the hiding place, hoping Tum will return safely with Juni's help.

Ulla Thynell
Ada-Ji
N
E
S
W

Magic

The action of heat is always present,
it penetrates all bodies and spaces,
it influences the processes of the arts,
and occurs in all the phenomena of the universe.

—John Baptiste Joseph Fourier,
The Analytical Theory of Heat, 1822

Act 1

ROCKS

Whiffs of burning wood wafted into her bedroom. Stretching, Dime changed out of her gown and wandered into the common area.

Dayn was kneeling on a pillow, holding a hot poker against the beams of a wooden chair. Its large metal wheels leaned, detached, against the table, which had been pushed to the side.

"Is this for our child or for the Light?" Dime asked. She was touched at the love her spouse was putting into the new wheelchair, but also worried at the number of times he'd traveled to the village for parts. They were supposed to be hiding.

"If it were for the Light, I'd be done by now." He stood, placing the iron back into the stove and waving his hand a bit. "Just a few more rounds, and I'll be ready to assemble it."

Dime circled the wooden arms and back, admiring the intricate geometric pattern Dayn had been carefully burning into them. Her first instinct was to ask why he wasn't woodburning *outside*, but considering their rather heated discussion after his last trip to the village, she was glad he was staying out of view.

IC dens, such as the one they were in, were concealed into the landscape, usually dug into the side of a plateau or a hillside, marked on the outside by a rock pattern known only to agents. The purpose of these dens was to house agents while they staged surveillance on outlying villages, gathering Intelligence on the pyrsi living there or checking on reported situations.

When she was younger, Dime had accepted these missions as normal business, but now, older and having better seen the many facets of society and government, she viewed them with less comfort. Maybe if the Circles wanted to know what its own pyrsi were doing, they should just ask them. And if an entire village was willing to hide something from the Circles, maybe that was their right.

"I know you're still worried about the supplies," Dayn said. "But we all needed things, I mean, who knows how long we'll be here? I was not eating one more tin of that mystery dein." Dime had to agree that the mushy preserved substance they'd scooped from the metal canister was most disturbing. "And if your friend carries Tum back,"—his casual tone did not belie his deep worry for their youngest—"we need to be ready for her."

Dayn was right; they'd needed supplies. The den was stocked with food, but only the sort that could keep for cycles. Luja had actively cheered when Dayn returned with fresh orangecobs. But it wasn't just the food, or the one trip.

Dime had also wanted a few additions to Ella's old climbing set, even though she knew where the pseudo-stairwell in the cliff was now. And Dayn wasn't going to build a wheelchair without the right metals and tools. But he'd since been into the village three more times, picking up additional pieces he'd later realized he needed.

As the village wasn't large, he couldn't just whisk in and out of a shop. Some parts had to be custom-forged, others improvised from what was available. He'd been seen a lot, and especially with his distinct city accent, they must have questioned where he was staying.

She knew they couldn't abide a life in hiding. But the plan was to get here and sort things out; Dime had hoped they could've kept a flat profile for a *little* while. Her family just wasn't used to living that way. Nor, she conceded, should they be.

Dayn's casual mention of "her friend" tugged at her. He'd trusted Dime when she said they could trust Juni to carry Tum off.

Dime had lived with the newts, and seen that they were complex and kind. To most anyone else, they were fictional beasts, used as a warning in ch'pyrsi's tales to encourage good behavior. Dime would never use such tactics to raise her own children, but she'd heard the tales growing up in school. Certainly, Dayn had as well.

Thus, when out of nowhere, a large, feathered creature with scaly arms had bounded toward him, and Dime had asked him on faith to let the howling newt carry their precious child away, it had not been trivial that he'd agreed.

They couldn't know whether Tum was safe. Dime had coped with the uncertainty by picturing her having a great time, keeping Juni company, with Agni bouncing around all the while. But this was a fantasy in her mind.

Her life had turned into a fantasy. With no stop to the sudden changes since the fairies had first entered her home, she felt disconnected, like she was searching for a way to belong again. Where was home for a wingless fairy?

On top of that, she'd learned wings weren't necessary to conduct valence; at least, that's what Ella thought. Ella had urged her to travel to the diamond caves themselves, where she thought Dime could experiment safely, both aided and shielded by the surrounding diamonds. As odd as the idea of using a mythical treasure hoard for extra wheels was, Ella seemed serious about it.

She'd also warned that the Fo-ror could detect the strong use of valence; it was how they'd initially tracked Dime's lengthy toothcar ride to the cliff. Still, she struggled with the idea of going right under the Seats' noses to hide from them. On the other hand, it would also allow her to follow up on her promise to Rock.

With that idea drawing her back, debating the rest of it was a bit moot.

Dime knew she needed to go soon, before another incident forced the valence from her—like the fissure she'd created outside Lodon— and put pyrsi in danger. The idea of putting pyrsi in danger had eaten at Dime's sleep as much as knowing Rock was still there, alone.

She knew she'd been stalling here, staying more than a turn and a half since Ella's departure. She'd needed it. Finally able to spend time with Dayn and their older child, Luja, she'd not felt able to race off into the unknown. Or maybe, like Dayn, she was hoping Tum would come back; then she could see her child here, safe, before leaving.

Also, the valence she'd used outside of Lodon had taken a great deal from her. Not just physical energy—it had also rattled her mind. If she was going to sneak into the most sacred place in the Heartland, she couldn't go in muddled or upset. Nor should she expose herself to its amplifying diamonds without a clearer mind. Not while seeing repeated images of the crack she'd made in the rocks themselves, of the contorted faces of Sol's Pillars shouting at her family, or of the pyr howling in fear as he was pulled from the crevice.

So she'd stayed, resting, trying to regain a sense of calm and stability, and making preparations for her trip. She'd repacked her backpack, with just essentials this time, in addition to her climbing supplies and a certain piece of art she and Luja had assembled.

The time to delay was over, so she wished she could pinpoint what was holding her back. There was another weight on her, one she couldn't name.

She froze, hearing a knock at the door, immediately replaced by a thrill as she recognized its distinct pattern. Nearly tumbling over each other, Dime and Dayn rushed up the stairs, as Luja made sarcastic comments that they fully ignored.

"Ador!" they called in unison as their best friend emerged.

Dime stopped, seeing someone behind him. "Hi, who's this?"

Ador stepped aside, revealing a smiling pyr. "This is Ma'Hin; he's been easing much of the work on my ledger. I don't know what I would have done lately without him. Oh, and he helped me drive here." Ador winked. Dime felt slightly less secure with a stranger here, after what she'd seen in the city, but it was a long drive, she knew, and Ador wasn't getting younger either.

Sadness gripped her, and embarrassment also. How much

had she been through that now her first reaction to a new face was unease? The Violence took so much more away than she'd ever considered. She offered Hin a smile, which he returned.

"Hin, welcome," Dayn said. "Here, let's get downstairs."

She pushed back her own feelings of trauma, realizing in a burst of joy—Ador was really here! So much had happened in the several turns since she'd seen him. Reaching the bottom of the staircase, she stepped back as the others joined her.

Luja stood at the table, beaming at Ador. "Hin, this is our child, Ji'Luja," Dayn said. "Luja, this is Ma'Hin; he's with the Free Winds." Luja stood and fanned vis fingers in what Dime thought to be a quite diplomatic way. Ve was too cute.

"Hello, Ador's friends," Hin greeted, ducking with a nervous bow. "I hope I'm not intruding. Ador's been letting me work with him lately, and, Burge, it's such an honor to meet you." He'd turned to Dime for the last bit.

"Me?" she blurted. *An honor?* Dime was pretty sure she was a full fugitive at this point.

"Um, yes. Leaving the Circles—it's good to see a pyr stand up like that. And then attacked by the fairies, but you were so brave and got away. It's just so nice to meet you." The young ma'pyr's eyes glimmered with sincerity, and Dime wasn't sure how to respond.

"We're glad to meet you too," Dayn said with a broad smile, beckoning the younger ma'pyr over to the table. "After all that's happened, we're especially grateful to have the Free Winds' support. We've known Ador a long time."

Ador grinned at Dime, who felt a bit of the weight lifting as she grinned back.

"What can I get you?" Dayn hustled around the small room, taking everyone's requests for food and drink as Dime pulled the table out where they could at least get the seats around it.

"That chair is really well done," Hin noted, pointing at Dayn's still-smoking masterpiece.

Dayn turned back from the stove. "Yes, it's for our other child,

Fe'Tum. She's staying with friends, but she'll be back soon. And Batu, she's well?"

Ador smiled, as he always did when his spouse was mentioned. "Yes, she is. She's trying to actively recruit, in the city. She hopes that with the Circles worried about the Pillars, they won't notice her efforts. She was so glad to see Dime, and she told me to send the rest of you her best regards."

He continued a while longer, updating Luja about what sounded like a counseling program ve must have recently had been working on with Batu, specially designed sessions on topics not discussed at the enclaves.

Her child, organizing political efforts—and Dime didn't even know. She resolved to ask Luja more when they had time, but Luja had pulled up a chair and was asking Hin and Ador all sorts of questions verself.

Dime glanced again around the table. Dayn was still by the stove, but she thought she could hear him humming under his breath. He and Ador always had been a special type of friends, the type that sought each other time and time again, no matter what life threw at them. Ador was dressed as elegantly as always, in a slate blue suit with wide, velvet trim. His tattoos of waves ran over his scalp, face, and neck like a fine sketchpiece.

Luja leaned forward, vis book abandoned on the side table, trying to get the pyr—who was close to an auncle—to pay attention to ver. Ve was wearing the same suit as when they'd left, a snug fit of different textures of purple. Off to their side, Hin wore a modern suit of thin fabric, in a smoky blue color.

Compared to the lot of them, Dime had to admit her loose black velour was four ways of drab. She still didn't care. Simple was the new fancy, she'd told an irritated Luja on more than one occasion. She did have her necklace, of course, but now that she knew what power it held, that was staying hidden. In fact, only a few pyrsi even knew she had it—some of them here—and now she was grateful she'd had that discretion.

Oh! She skipped back into her room, and came out with arms held behind her back. "I have something for you!"

Ador grinned with mock exasperation. "Former Agent Dime. I am allowed to give you a celebratory gift without you finding me something in return. I told you; I was proud of you."

"Hey, so I swung by the Fo-ror city and picked this up for you. No big deal." Dime almost bounced as she held out the case, which she'd kept wrapped in a soft towel until now.

Appearing speechless—which Dime quite enjoyed—Ador fumbled around the smooth dark wood case, looking for a latch. As he slowly pulled from both sides, the box opened in the middle, revealing a multi-level hinged game board that unfolded and popped up in places as it stretched. Game board was an inadequate term for it. The detailed carvings were more like a sculpture, a miniature forest with platforms, branches, and dangling ropes.

Dime practically giggled.

Though the design was mostly wood without any superfluous felt or such, artfully placed touches of dark green paint created the illusion of much more green than there was: a tiny forest kingdom in one small box.

Ador still hadn't reacted. Dime clapped as he turned the game around. "There's a drawer in the back, with pieces," she said, pointing. "There are little carved squips, flat tokens, and a set of dice. I mean, just six-sided dice, not like those treasures you gave me." Dime patted her pocket.

Ador found the drawer and pulled out one of the wooden squips, its little tail carved as realistically as though it were sitting on his finger.

"Awww!" Luja clapped. "That's so cute." Ador handed it to ver, and ve turned it around and around in vis fingers. "So how do you play it?"

Dime threw her hands to both sides. "No idea! I got a little wrapped up on my way out and it didn't come with rules."

"I bet Lu can come up with some," Ador said with a wink.

"For sure. Maybe not exact, but we'll figure it out." Luja was scanning the intricate board like it was a patient. "Here, Hin," ve gestured. "Come over here and let's work it out." With a nod from Ador, Luja moved the game to the square side table, leaning vis book against the wall.

Dime wished ve would be more careful with vis books.

A silence caught her, and she scanned around the table. Hin hadn't responded to Luja, and his eyes were turned to the side, fixed on the game.

Ador glanced between them, as if realizing something. His eyes met Dime's, offering her a quick apology. "So, even in the Free Winds, we have some divided ideas about the fairies. Hin, it must be a shock to hear that pyrsi are having contact with them. I think, though, the more we learn about them, the more possibilities it will open."

Oh. Whoops. Batu had said the Free Winds discussed the fairies in a positive light, but it must have been jarring for Dime to pop out that she'd swung by the Heartland. And maybe Hin hadn't been part of those particular discussions. She should have been more careful, but it was hard balancing the familiarity of their dear friend with the sensitivity of a new face. She supposed Ador dealt with this all the time.

"Hin," she said, trying to sound reassuring, "when the fairies came for me, it wasn't something I expected. This has all been unexpected. I'm just trying to deal with it. We all are." A thought occurred to her, as a flash of anxiety returned. "You probably heard about what happened outside the city."

"I heard Sol's Pillars tried to stop you, but you got away again."

"The rumors are all over the place," Ador added. "Some say the fairies showed up and attacked you again, others say you attacked them. Others insist the Sol's Pillars got out of hand and are now making up wild stories to deflect attention. Some even say you rose up on a mountain, like the story of Sol."

She threw Ador a warning look. If Hin wasn't sure yet about the fairies, she wasn't about to reveal any more of her secrets just yet. She turned to Hin.

"The Sol's Pillars did . . . become aggressive." She didn't want to say that they'd breached the line of the Violence. She hoped she wasn't like the Circles, denying the truth to make things easier. But right now, escalation was on her mind.

Hin leaned forward. "One thing Ador has taught me is the importance of free discussion. I'm not sold on the fairies, but the Free Winds are united in one thing—the Violence cannot return."

They all murmured in assent, Dayn glancing over from where he was mixing ingredients in a bowl. He gave her a smile.

"The Pillars don't seem to get that," Hin added, looking up at her. "I'm sorry how they treated you. But we're here, now, and you're with us. Right? I mean, part of the Free Winds?" He sat up taller.

"I am," she said. "I mean, I'd like to be. So, we're here. Tell me about the Free Winds, anyway." She looked at Ador. "From your perspective," she clarified. "I know what the IC thinks."

Hin relaxed, his intensity softening as he scooted over to sit with Luja at the side table. Luja fumbled a little squip, scrambling to catch it before it hit the table. Ve gave Dime an apologetic grimace.

She hoped Ador didn't mind her asking so directly. But she'd really been berating herself these last turns for how she'd allowed his work to stay separate from their friendship. It wasn't just the information he'd now have and how they might work together, but when she'd visited Batu she'd understood—what Ador did was part of who he was. She hoped he'd forgive her for that lack of insight.

Ador returned a sad smile, like more was on his mind. "Some call the Free Winds an organization or a faction," he began. She wondered how many times he'd had to give this speech. "I prefer to describe it as conversation space—an open field where ideas and projects can seed and grow. There is no badge or pledge required. We simply bring pyrsi together to enable them to discuss our challenges and needs, as well as ways the Circles could better address them. And then those of us without ambitions of rank take those ideas and present them to the Circles for consideration.

"Sometimes I'm asked what good we've done." Ador's reactions were often subtle, but Dime could tell from his slight tensing how much this idea distressed him. "Fact is, we've spent cycles upon cycles just socializing the idea that pyrsi should talk about the issues that affect them—just getting pyrsi to face their fears about speaking. We still have no hold within the Circles, who only tell us such changes are not possible. All we have is a growing number of pyrsi willing to talk at all. To state what they want, what they need. It's still an accomplishment, or at least Batu insists that it is."

Dime wanted to discuss the Fo-ror with him. Hin was clearly uncomfortable with the subject, but if their goal was to open minds through dialogue, there was no better time to start. "What do you know about the Fo-ror?"

Ador met her gaze. "Not enough. We have some who have been . . . close to their lands. We have a few scraps, a few documents. And, still, we only discuss them in smaller groups. Pyrsi we know won't send Enforcement after us or throw up a flag." Dime had a feeling he was originally going to finish with *to the IC*, but this didn't upset her.

Seeming to process her reaction, he sat a stride, tapping on the table. "You've been there. You really have. That's incredible. How much you could share."

"Well, I had an idea on that. So—I'm planning to go back." She glanced to check Hin's reaction, but he and Luja were busy deciphering the game.

"He'll be fine," Ador said under his breath. "It's an adjustment."

"You're telling me." The tension finally breaking, they both laughed. Dime sat back in her chair. "I could reach out to someone there and ask if they'd be willing to meet here. Trust me," she said, thinking of the clunky climbing gear loaded in her bag, "it's easier for the Fo-ror to reach us than it is for us to reach them."

"It makes me question," Dayn said from behind Ador, wiping his hands on a towel, "why they haven't before?"

"A few reasons," Dime answered. "Mostly, the same propaganda that drives us to stay away. 'The Ja-lal are brutes.' They call us brutes, you know. 'The brutes crave resources and build machines. The brutes love the Violence and would return it in a snap, if they weren't inferior'—as they see it."

"I can understand why that keeps them away. It keeps us away," Luja said from the table. Of course ve'd continued to listen.

"Yes," Dime said, turning toward ver and Hin, now both listening. "But it's worse." She looked back at Ador. "It's worse. The main reason they don't come here is they think there's nothing to come here for. Do you know what they call Sol's Reach?"

"Uppergrowth?" Dayn asked, a sizzling sound emerging on the stove behind him.

Dime almost chuckled. "No. The Barrens. They call our home the Barrens, and that's how they see it."

"I would like you to request their visit," Ador said, sitting straighter. "It would be a great honor to join in that conversation. I mean, we've talked to Fo-ror elsewhere, but it's not the same. Different characters, too hard to read."

Dime had a sudden visual image. This time, she did chuckle. "No one's too chatty at the Crossing, you mean? No, I can attest to that."

Ador sat back. "My friend." He slowly shook his head.

"I know. Let's just . . . accept that things are different now. I've seen a lot. I've heard a lot." She couldn't imagine what he was going to say when he heard her full story, though maybe not right here, with the stove sizzling and Hin and Luja clattering the little squips around. She hoped they were being careful.

"Ma-ma, I was thinking something about wings," Luja said. "About what you said about the composition, and—" Dime didn't think ve'd talk about her story without her permission, but maybe with Ador here, ve felt comfortable. It wasn't Luja's news to break.

"We'll talk about it later?"

Luja's mouth suspended a moment, as if ve was hoping Dime

would let ver continue. Instead, ve shrugged and went back to sorting game pieces.

Dayn walked over to the table, setting down a plate of flatcakes. "I can say one thing," he offered, blinking back a moment of emotion. "I'm so grateful to be here with each of you. And Hin, thank you for joining us. You're always welcome."

Hin fanned his fingers and accepted the cakes that Dayn slid onto a plate.

Dime knew, looking around at the pyrsi she'd desperately wanted to find, that soon she was going to leave them again.

"Hello?" Ador's face poked through the open door. The smell of smoke crept in from the main area; Dayn must be woodburning again. Dime had crashed onto the bed after the meal, and hadn't yet felt like getting up. *Wait.* She glanced around for Hin, and relaxed again, seeing that it was just her friend. Hin seemed to be warming up here, but they hadn't reached bed-chat level yet.

"Come on in."

Ador closed the door behind him then sat next to her, letting out a long sigh. He leaned over, as if noticing something.

"What?" By instinct, Dime shifted back.

"Diamond. You are growing hair."

"What?" Dime ran her hand back over her scalp, feeling the soft little pricks bend under her fingers. "Oh. Yes, it's very strange. I've shaved by the bells forever, but ever since I got back, I've just sort of forgotten."

"I'm so proud of you."

"For the hair? For not dying?" The dying joke caused her immediate guilt, remembering Zael back in Lodon. She wasn't sure whether Ador knew him or not.

"For deciding to be you."

"Well, I've realized I was always me. I think that was the problem."

Ador lay down next to her on the bed's overcover. "Honestly, I'm just glad you're ok. It would be nice to not think about all this for a while, but I don't think we can."

Exhaustion and frustration had been stirring in Dime, and Ador's words tapped right into that. She was tired of secrets, and sneaking, and justifying crap she hadn't caused, and her friend was here and she wanted him to understand. "Yeah. It's all changing. And I can't stop feeling like I keep making it worse and I don't know how to fix any of it. Sometimes I wish I could just get out. Like, not be the center of all this."

"I don't know what you've been through. But I want to help."

Dime absolutely knew he was curious to ask why she'd been the one attacked, but he was too polite to ask it. Lamenting the brevity of their carefree moment, she sat up.

"I'm a Fo-ror, Ador. Physically. One of their leaders crafted some terrible scheme to overtake the Ja-lal. He . . . cut my wings off when I was a ba'pyr, and left me near the Circles, hoping I'd grow up there and gain influence." There was no one in the world, other than Dayn, that Dime wanted to just *believe* her.

After a long silence, he sat up and offered his arms. "Come here," he said, and sitting next to him, Dime relaxed against his shoulder. He rocked her back and forth, and Dime breathed dry tears into the shoulder pad of his soft, tailored suit. "I'm so sorry."

"Thanks," she said. "Dayn keeps telling me it's ok, but maybe I needed someone to agree it was a little not ok too."

"I know," he said. She couldn't read his expression when he gazed over at her, his hands lifting from her shoulders.

"I think I can perform valence anyway," she continued, feeling relief, for once, to get it all out. "And when we left town. It really was me that made . . . the fissure that allowed us to leave." That was tough for her to talk about, but it was just Ador here, she reminded herself. "I mean, not a mountain; I'm not *that* good."

Dime reached for her pendant and pulled it from her shirt. "Diamonds collect valence, I'm told. And I've been wearing it a long time without using it. Ella—she's a friend I've met—thinks I have a lot of power.

"I don't want power, but it's tuned to me. I can't give it away. So I can ignore it and continue to let it endanger pyrsi, or I can try to use it to help. I've decided. I'm going back to the Heartland to see what I can learn."

Ador continued to nod slowly, like a ch'pyr's toy. She *was* throwing a lot at him. Perhaps too much. "I'd trust Ella's instincts," he finally said.

Dime hadn't imagined Ador knew Ella. Goodness. "Can we talk about all of it?"

"Of course," he said. Reading her mind, he flopped back onto the bed. Joining him with an equally silly flop, back and forth they poured out their stories, their fears, and their hopes.

Gazing up at the ceiling as they talked, Dime vowed to keep one thing in mind. The most precious thing she possessed was, without question, her friends.

At this point, she was pretty much a pro climbing down the cliff. Though she did need to stop doing so in the dark. Even with all her stalling, she hadn't wanted to wait until daylight, as the Seats' complex was less attended pre-dawn, and she wanted to give herself the best chance of not causing a stir. *Heh.*

Avoiding stirs would be no easy feat, given that she had to enter the Seats' complex just to get into the diamond caves. At least, Dime didn't know of any other entrances. Besides, she needed to go that way. She had a stop to make.

Climbing was easier now that she knew where the rough staircase was in the cliff, and it also would take her right to the edge of the city, so she wouldn't have to search this time. Glad for the reflection of the nightlight off of the ledges, and letting her natural vision guide her, Dime descended each section of the cliff in turn.

"There's probably a reason pyrsi take the extra time to go through the Crossing," she muttered to a twittering bird, bounding across a cliffside branch. "But then, those pyrsi probably have a *car*."

She'd left the den not long after her talk with Ador. Seeing him, she'd now realized, had given her a boost she'd subconsciously needed. Maybe related to why she'd been stalling. Spouses were the best companions, and great motivation for staying—but sometimes it was the jolt of a friend that got a pyr back up and out the door, ready to try a thing again.

With fondness, Dime remembered their faces as she'd left.

Ador had beamed like a teacher watching a star student joining a career. Friendship aside, this irritated her more than a little, though not in any serious way. She was substantially younger than the pyr, who was just barely in his Dorh, but she wasn't a ch'pyr either.

Even more, he'd told Hin her now almost-noticeable hair was a sign of defiance against doctrine, and so the young pyr had continued to glance up at her scalp in admiration as he wished her safe travels.

Luja had been almost as enthusiastic, repeating over and over in stilted sentences how awesome vis mother was, clearly trying to make sure ve didn't blurt Dime's secret, with Hin standing right there, wide-eyed. "You're . . . awesome . . . because!" ve continued to say, finally launching into a huge hug then running off with a sniffle.

Dayn had been the most reserved at her departure, keeping his arms folded and offering a tight, forced smile under sad eyes. As stoic as he was, he didn't look ready to be without her again, not with the stress of Tum's absence always on his mind. Dime trusted Juni; she felt in her very being that Tum was safe. But that was not an easy thing to tell a fretting father—in fact she'd be just as scared, in his shoes.

She wished she could stay with him too. At a loss for words herself, she'd given him a lingering kiss on the cheek, hoping it said them for her. Then, determined to stick to her plan, she'd trudged off into the nightlight, reflecting down from the skystones. And here she was again.

Dime reached the floor of the Heartland and, sitting down a stride, tucked the climbing supplies down the back edge of her bag.

She could have followed the cliff directly to the complex, but Dime had been serious about finding someone to meet with Hin and Ador. Ador had been serious too. He'd decided to stay at the den, wanting no risk of missing the meeting, though he seemed to need a break from the city anyway. And with Hin there, Luja would have someone vis age to keep ver company. Until the meeting, anyway.

She didn't know what could come of it, just a few pyrsi in between two powerful governments, but Da-da had always told her, "If you don't know what to do, try talking with someone."

Her instincts returned to the fairy who, in the brief time Dime had interacted with her, had been kind, strong, and had seen that Dime had no wings and yet not called her out. There was an independent spirit to her that felt right for this. Dime thought she had a chance at finding this fairy again.

Keeping note of her surroundings, Dime pushed through the brush, moving forward until she came upon the canal where she'd entered the first time. Cleared on both sides, it reminded her of a lowcity alley, lined by trees rather than walls. As she edged along its nor bank without any disguise or concealment, she took the time she needed to pass each section and ensure, as best she could, that she wasn't seen.

A few pyrsi were seated, leaning against the remnants of a stone structure. "Pardon?" Dime whispered from the shadows. She hoped her accent didn't sound too strange, or at least that they weren't worrying about it. "Have you seen Uchitar around here lately?" She'd meant to ask for Volana directly, but remembering how the fairy had been insulted by some of the others, caution stayed her.

"Uchitar? You think he'd drag up so far this way?" Xe waved a dismissive arm in the direction of Pito.

"Leave him alone," another said, in a higher-pitched voice. "He has enough issues without your grief."

"Mind your role," the first snapped. "It's just his pusher, anyway, don't know why you'd want to help xem. But if you're so into it,"—xe turned back in Dime's direction then back around when xe saw she was hidden—"just follow the creek and you'll trip over him eventually."

Dime continued past, wanting to say she wasn't anyone's pusher, but knowing just speaking here was a liability. She kept a careful watch as she moved along the dark trees, following the sheen of the skystones over the creek. Probably natural in origin, but leveled and smoothed by the masons, it reminded her of similar work the Construction Circle performed on the ravines of Lodon.

It worried her that Uchitar might be flying, and she might miss him. Or maybe he'd gone somewhere else entirely. Ella had said Pito was at least as populated as Lodon and even more spread out. If he'd left, she couldn't take the time or risk right now to keep searching. Dime wasn't lacking the skill or patience, but she couldn't chance the Seats knowing she was back before she reached the caves. That was critical to her plans.

Dime almost tripped over Uchitar.

The good side was that he appeared to be alone. The bad side was that she couldn't tell if he was asleep or unconscious. Again, she lamented Luja's absence. Dime was sure she'd learned what to do with an unconscious pyr at some point, in some class. It was all muddled now. Luja would have known.

"Uchitar," she said, feeling that any formalities would just come across as condescending. "Uchitar." She leaned in, trying to see whether he was breathing.

He was, but his body jerked in unnatural motions. She worried over his twitching body, his bruised arms, his weakly flapping wings. She spoke his name again and again, but he didn't answer. In a flash of panic, a spark flew from her fingers. Uchitar shot upright, almost knocking her over.

"Good Sha!" He stared at Dime. "Are you back or is this a weird dream?"

Dime was still staring at her fingers, fear creeping through them into her arms like a physical force. She wasn't sure what she'd done, but her ability to reach the valence—if that's really what it was—had definitely grown since the incident outside the city. She could have hurt him. She needed to get to those caves and figure it out.

"Um, I'm back. Fe'Dime." She added her name just in case he'd forgot. She thought about apologizing for shocking him, but he didn't seem to know it had happened. Telling him might shock him again, though this time without the literal spark. And she wasn't eager to explain to a stranger what she couldn't explain to herself. "Please don't tell anyone," she added.

Uchitar groaned and leaned back against his bony hands. "*Uhhhhhhh.* I feel awful."

Dime stopped herself from responding that he looked it, too. "Are you ok? Can I get you anything?"

"I can manage." His expression softened. "Thank you for checking. Are all you brutes this nice?"

"Oh, there's lots of surprises in the world, you'll find. And no. I'm a unique brew."

Uchitar laughed, which turned into spitting something mucousy from his mouth. Dime edged back. "Sorry," he said, flapping over to the creek before returning. She still wasn't used to watching them use their wings just to leap a short distance. *Such power.*

"So, uh, why me? I'm not hallucinating, right? It wouldn't be the first time, so I just need to be sure."

"No, I'm here. But, I suppose a hallucination could say that too."

"Nope. They just talk. Never answer."

"Well, if you're really fine for now, I do need to get going."

"I'll live." He paused. "Take care. Stop in anytime."

Dime stifled a chuckle, though the reaction made her feel guilty. His situation wasn't funny, yet the pyr was warm and endearing. She wished she could help him, that they could laugh together.

"I'm sorry, I didn't mean I was leaving this stride, but I do need to go soon. And I didn't answer you, actually. 'Why you?' you asked. I don't know, you were just a pyr I knew how to find?" While true, Dime immediately regretted the explanation as Uchitar's face drew. "I mean, I trust you. Or maybe we were meant to find each other. There's big changes going on in the world. Bigger problems."

"And you're looking to a junkie to fix them?"

Dime winced at the slur. "Right now, I'm looking at you. And your friend, Volana, does she come around?" She didn't want to admit so directly that she'd been trying to locate Volana. Uchitar's eyes had lit a little at the idea that she needed his help. They'd lit like he was someone who would want to be part of a solution, and Dime wasn't going to dissuade him from that.

Except . . . was she ready to potentially place the odds of war in the hands of a pyr whose current best contribution was *not* throwing up in the creek? Maybe she was being too open.

"Volana?" He didn't seem troubled by the question; in fact, a smile broke at her mention. "She's Sha with wings, if you ask me. I mean, don't tell her I said that. But, could I ask you . . . what's this all about?"

Dime smiled now too. "That's a great question. I've had a run-in with your Seats. I'd like to clear it up before someone starts a war xe can't stop."

Uchitar shuddered at the mention of war. "That's something I'd want Volana for, too." He glanced out into the trees. "I don't know where she lives, but I've got her patterns down pretty well." He cut Dime a sharp look. "Don't take anything strange by that, I just have a lot of time down here lately. No one looks out for us like Volana. Here, let's go." He stood.

Wavering on shaky legs, Uchitar flapped his wings and rose into the air, tilting a little side to side. "Oh," he said. "You're really one of them, aren't you?" He landed with a bump. "I'm too weak to try and lift you. We'll have to walk."

Together, they wove through the tall trees, Dime breathing in all the scents of the forest, so much richer than any musk boutique. She was sure she'd never tire of them. They moved slowly, Uchitar wobbling as he walked. "There she is," he said.

As before, Volana tended to a group huddled beside the trunk of a massive tree. Dime couldn't get over the size of the trees here, how old they must be. "Stay here," Uchitar whispered. He stumbled out into the clearing and pulled Volana aside.

Dime watched them talk. Uchitar's robes were muddy and stained, and beside him Volana was like a patchwork rainbow, the variety of colorful ribbons bouncing and swaying from her robes, including her extended mid-section, with the look of an advanced pregnancy. Her long white braids bounced as they talked.

Volana bid farewell to the others and walked off with Uchitar. After a stride or two, Uchitar waved to Dime. She joined them, and Volana glanced at Dime's mostly bald, tattooed head, as if letting the truth of Dime's identity sink in.

"Hello, Dime, it's so good to see you." Volana curved her fingers with a wavy motion as her wings fluttered behind her. Dime enjoyed Volana's Fo-ror way of speaking, even more pronounced than Uchitar's. It reminded her of music.

"Hello, Volana." She fanned her fingers. "It's a complicated story, but I'm looking for someone here I can trust." Volana nodded, waiting for more. "So, there's been some contact between our societies. I don't know if you've heard anything here, but the Ja-lal are in an uproar about a few Fo-ror who flew into Lodon, our city." Volana clearly hadn't heard that, by her reaction.

"I'm here for reasons I can't tell anyone yet, but I'm trying to find someone to meet with my friends just over the cliff. Ja-lal friends. They're leaders in an organization that's open to talking with the Fo-ror. We don't have an agenda for the meeting—it would just be a chance to talk. We're all trying to figure things out, really. And prevent a misunderstanding turning into the Violence," she added.

"I would agree with that. But why are you talking to me?" Volana motioned back toward herself, as if pointing out something obvious.

Dime tried to remember what Ella had told her about Fo-ror class structure. It was even more ingrained than in Sol's Reach, she'd said. She'd warned Dime to remember that. She didn't have to agree with it, but she couldn't ignore its impact on the pyrsi here.

"Can I tell you a secret? I've met three of your Seats. I'm unimpressed. I need a Fo-ror who understands the heartbeat of your society, someone who is open-minded and will talk to my friends, even just to sort through ideas. Everyone here holds you in such high regard." Uchitar scrunched his face at this. "Would you go? And," she didn't want to leave him out, "perhaps Uchitar?"

Uchitar sputtered with bitter laughter.

"No," Dime said to both of them. "I'm serious. Why not you? Of course, if you aren't comfortable, maybe you can direct me to someone who would be."

Volana's stare was sharp. She hesitated before speaking. "I am also involved in such an organization. It is called the Foundry. We are a mix of pyrsi who meet in secret. We believe in offering the pyrsi . . . voice. I could get one of our higher-class leaders to assist you."

By the discomfort in Volana's tone, she was putting a lot of trust in Dime just by mentioning the Foundry. Dime appreciated that, and it gave her hope. "Why not you? I don't know these other leaders, but I've met and trust you. It's just a meeting, and for now, fewer pyrsi involved might be safer." In the hesitant way Volana had mentioned the Foundry, she thought the idea of discretion would resonate.

"Why not—" Volana repeated the words. "Fine. I will go, just to meet them. Uchitar, you're going with me."

Uchitar could not even pretend to look mad, though he did look uneasy.

"Of course," she amended, "only if you are willing. But—you will go?" She turned to Dime. "Tell us where."

"Yes, of course. Could you . . . provide some light?" Dime was curious whether she could make the stones glow herself, if she really did have valence. This wasn't the time to try, though.

The fairy lit a small stone, filling the area with light. Dime rummaged in her bag, finding her map. Pulling it out and unfolding just the sur edge, she showed Volana the location, in relation to the geography of the cliff. She explained the hidden entrance to the den and then put the map back in her bag. "My family is there also," she added. "One of my children, perhaps the other."

Volana offered a kind smile, understanding. "You can trust us with their location, Dime." She patted her midsection. "I will have a ba'pyr soon, if all goes well. I think maybe just this one. I am asexual, so—" she shrugged. "Who knows, maybe two. For now, one. I know what it feels like to want to protect. Even now."

"My father is aromantic." Dime wasn't sure why she offered the comparison, but Volana nodded, seeming to appreciate it. Uchitar had wrapped his arms around himself and was trembling.

"He needs more water," Volana explained. "He has so many troubles, this one. We are close, though. Are we not?" She leaned over, and Uchitar allowed her to peck a small kiss on his cheek. "You picked a good pyr. For your trust."

"I know I did," Dime answered. For all of their mutual respect, Dime didn't want to burden them with her destination. She'd put them at enough risk. "I need to go. I have a couple more things I need to do here before I return to the den myself."

"Yes," Volana said. "I have a shift to work, and Uchitar needs some care before we leave. As much as a turn, to rid his toxins." She looked downward, as if there were more to it than that. "Will that work for your friends?"

It will need to. "Yes, of course. I don't think they'll be leaving soon. And please, only the two of you? For now?"

Volana nodded, adding a warm smile. "Safe travels, Dime."

"To you as well," Dime said, and walked off again into the dark forest, the busy sounds of the city breaking through above her.

Dime managed to make it all the way to the rock walls behind which rested the Seats' complex and also, she now realized, the diamond caves. There was no longer one casual guard at the entrance, but several. None read books. There was no way to dart past them anymore, as she'd feared.

She'd repeated the plan in her mind on the way here, and she breathed in slowly, willing herself the resolve to go through with it. This might be her worst plan yet, but Dime could not pass through the complex without detection, nor could she walk in fully as herself yet. The compromise had been Luja's idea, and at the Aoch's continued insistence, Dime had finally agreed.

For once, she wanted to just be herself again. And soon, she would. There were still other pyrsi involved, she repeated. This wasn't just about her.

From the safety of the trees, Dime eased a large cloth bag out of her backpack, one that she would be glad to shed, for the bulk it added. She reshuffled the rest of her items in the backpack and slung it onto her shoulders.

Trying to minimize the jingles, she wriggled three items from the cloth bag: her mirror, a charcoal blush powder, and a glittering, metallic . . . well, she had no idea what to call it. Certainly the Fo-ror had names for things that went on their heads. It wasn't a hood, by any measure. She and Luja had worked on the masterpiece together: a giant mass of fabric strips, metallic rings, and little beads and grommets from construction work, sewn together onto a double-layered scarf that wrapped around her forehead and tied behind her neck.

It had felt so criminal building something to cover one's head, but she wasn't going to wear it in Sol's Reach, so why should anyone care? At Luja's suggestion, she'd modeled the dangling cords off of ones some Ja-lal dancers tied over their hips. She had no idea whether Fo-ror dancers had particular costumes, but, either way, maybe they'd invented the next big thing.

Holding the mirror in one hand, she tapped the gray blush

powder over her cheeks with the other. She disliked makeup, but it served, here, to diminish the prominence of the tattooed leaves that extended onto the sides of her cheeks. The dark gray powder, the only shade they'd had in the village, also made her look older. Not bad older; it was just a shock. She slid the powder into a pocket and stared at the cloth and metal . . . thing.

"Alright," she grumbled, "we made this work before. We can make it work again. I don't have Luja here this time, so be nice." The bundle of strings and metal bits did not respond. Dime reached for the fabric holding it together, and carefully wrestled it onto her head, tying it into position. She stood, slowly.

Finding her balance, she arranged the metallic strands so the short ones fell to the sides of her face, dangling over the rest of her tattoos and obscuring them in their shadows and distraction. A few strands hovered just above her eyes. And the longer ones draped over her backpack, creating such a display of shine and glitter, even in the nightlight, she hoped no one would bother to look whether there were wings folded behind. Or notice her rather ordinary black suit and flat shoes below, elements she had refused to replace.

She took a quick glance in the mirror, laughing despite herself. "Another day in the office!" She pushed the mirror into a pocket. If she was going to do this, she was going to do it right, and not let Luja down. *Here we go.*

Dime strode, with all the jingle she could muster, up to the guards. She drew out her words, exaggerating her accent as if it were an affectation. "Good morning! Is this the right entrance for the lounge?"

"The lounge? Burge, you must be in the wrong place."

"The wrong place? The clerk described it as here. This is where the private parties are. I dance." Dime swayed, letting her strands jingle.

One of the guards looked reluctant to leave xyr post; another walked over to join them. "What is this? I wasn't told about any party."

Dime was regretting this by the moment; she didn't even wear heels and here she was in full jingle. Maybe she shouldn't have let an Aoch form the plan. No, she couldn't let them see her discomfort. Dancers were always comfortable; it was something she admired in them. "Hmm, if this is the wrong place, I'll just go. I have plenty of places to dance. I just know Neimano would be so disappointed to hear I arrived but wasn't let in."

"Seat Neimano?" The guards exchanged concerned looks. All Dime could think about was Neimano flying her infant self to Lodon, and she didn't even have to act to appear flustered. Though, if she needed another distraction, there it was.

"Oh! Should I not say his name? He and I have a most unique relationship going back many, many cycles. He has cradled me in his arms and together we fl—"

"Burge, that's enough." Xe cleared xyr throat. Dime understood; a pyr wouldn't be able to unsee thoughts of the sneering Neimano's intimate moments. "Please, let one of us go in and find you an escort. We'll find someone who can accompany you, and make sure you're in the right place."

"I don't have time for that." She gave a haughty flip of her head, immediately hoping it wouldn't knock the scarf off. Relieved that it stayed in place, she turned to leave, taking care not to angle her back directly toward the guards. Glancing around, she saw they were shielding their eyes at the twinkle of her embellishments against the bright glowstones. She crouched slightly, the same way she'd seen Uchitar do when he was about to fly.

"No, wait," one guard called. "Here, you know where the lounge is?"

"Of course I do! Surely you don't want me to say out here, but once inside the private area, lounge is in a side room off the first passage. Big, carved doors. Green sofas." She wasn't exactly sure how to get to the hidden tapestry entrance since a High Guard had been snuffing the lights out last time she was escorted back there, but she hoped the small detail of the Seats' private area lent credibility.

"What did you say your name was?"

She smiled, as big a smile as she could muster. *"Fe'Diamond."* She winked. One of the guards chuckled. One started to follow her in, and she waved a hand. "I'm fine; I know the way. Stay at your post and watch for trouble."

"Do you promise . . . someone is expecting you here?"

Before recent events, Dime hadn't considered how much the honor of promises depended solely on the pyr offering them, not on any sort of core truth, as she'd been taught. This guard clearly held by them. As did Dime.

She tried to look offended. "I promise someone is waiting for me inside. Someone *most important* with whom I have shared many long, sweltering—"

"Burge, I've got it. Take care."

"You as well." Elated she'd actually been believable as a dancer, Dime started to sing as she walked through the corridors. She'd learned on her last visit that the Seats usually convened with the daylight, so she figured those here would be workers, maintainers, the types not present while the Chambers were in session. As a pretty decent singer, she kept on as she strolled the long hallways.

Pyrsi passed her, some grinning at her attention-grabbing costume, and others whisking by, irritated by the distraction or with their jobs on their minds. Not wanting any more accidental encounters with High Guards—or, Sol forbid, the Seats them-selves—Dime kept to the outer corridors, as best she remembered them.

With more caution and no longer singing, she reached the dark, plain passages where the prison cells began. She knew the guards here stayed away for bells at a time, but she didn't want to run into them if her timing was poor.

Dime stopped near the entrance to the front cells, listening intently for any sound. Not hearing anything, she eased down the hallway, nervous about her own tiny jingles, but not yet ready to shed their protection. Not until one critical thing had been done.

She knew she'd only get one chance. If that. She was glad to see a series of empty cages. Except for one.

Rock was sitting cross-wise on the bed, a blade and a chunk of wood in her hand, when Dime approached. She wished she could bottle and sell the look on her face.

"Holy killstroke, D." Rock, for the first time since Dime had met her, was at a loss for words. Dime first took a stride to enjoy that.

"I know! I just walked in this way." She giggled. "Even told them my name. Here, we have important business. Will any guards be by soon?"

"No." Rock continued to stare.

Dime glanced into her cell. It was filled with small wooden carvings of mountain birds. One large owl caught her eye, which then moved to the large blade. "They gave you a blade?"

"They don't think I'm going to return the Violence, D, they just think I want to escape. Besides, now I can at least shave. She tapped the top of her head. These pyrsi never *shave*."

"Well, you *are* going to escape," Dime said, avoiding the moment when Rock noticed Dime's own growing hair. "But why carved birds?"

"Turns out, the pyrsi here *love* them. Passes the time, too. I've been taking all sorts of requests. The workers sneak back and tell me what they'd like. In exchange, they bring me little baked goods and candies. Never really had a sweet tooth, but it violates their ethics or whatever if they don't bring me something, and let's face it—it's a small cage."

"I love that owl," Dime blurted.

"Sol, D, you can have it. It's not for anyone anyway. Just something I carved while thinking of you."

Dime squinted. "Thanks. But we don't have time for this. You're ready to go, right?"

"I've been ready to go . . . anyway." Rock gestured toward the cage's bars. "You have a plan?"

Beaming, Dime unsnapped her valuables pouch and pulled out

Guard Wayniam's diamond-accented key, holding it before her like an enchanted scepter in a story.

Rock's expression fell. "No, I told you, those are tuned to the guard who carries them. It's a valence thing. Only Wayniam can use it, and he hasn't even been back since you left."

Dime hadn't thought that through. Keys fit locks, not pyrsi; it's how she'd always seen them. Well, she wasn't going to stand here and worry about it when she could just find out. Breathing in, she pushed the key into the lock and willed it to open. Nothing happened. She concentrated on the device inside the latch, and . . . coaxed it. She wanted to get Rock out of here. She thought about that.

The latch popped open, and Rock hurriedly pushed the door to swing it open. "Maybe I'll figure that out later," the agent said, blinking. "See, stealing pays off."

"I didn't steal it, I borrowed it, and I'll leave it right here. Can I really have that owl?"

"Hurt, yes, here." Rock handed her the owl, which fell, heavy, in Dime's hands. "I'm not carrying it. Now, you *are* going to take that off, right?"

Rock helped Dime untie the huge heavy covering. She sat it down on the floor of the cell, where its long strands swept out over the floor.

"Hey, not in here. I need to pack."

"Oh." Dime dragged the clinking, jingling mass out into the hall.

"Make more noise," Rock offered.

"Sorry."

The fact was, the covering did Dime no good at this point. Even though Rock didn't have tattoos—an extreme rarity in Sol's Reach— the two of them together without wings or hair would be hard to miss. Rock was free of the diamond cage. And Dime was done with costumes. *Done.*

"Rock?"

"Yes?" Rock looked amused as she packed up her items, and a few of the birds, into a small bag.

"I've got more news for you, but not here. I'm about to try something extremely risky and dangerous. If you want to get back to Sol's Reach, I can tell you where there's a—"

"If you're staying around, I'm staying with you." Rock looked up. "I mean, if I'm welcome. You know, you're basically a desk-master now. You might need a little help."

Dime grinned. "Come on, let's both get out of this killstink cage; it's creeping me out just being here again. And Rock? Let's not return."

"Deal." Rock reached into a pocket and pulled out a pod of cosmetic paint, which she smeared across her lips, restoring them to a bright, shiny blue. She smacked both lips together, making a loud *pop*. "Let's get out."

"So, we're not actually going *out* yet."

"*What?*"

"More . . . *in*. Further into the cliff. I'm going to the diamond caves. You still up?"

"Whatever. Let's get the harm away from this thing." Rock choked back sudden tears. She stopped as soon as she started, throwing Dime a warning look not to talk about it.

The needle on Dime's wristpiece was wiggling, yet it pointed clearly down the hall, away from where they'd first entered. As they walked down it together, several passageways emerged to one side. Through them, Dime could hear voices.

"From what I understand, those are all the regular prison areas," Rock said. "Most pyrsi get thrown in for a while for minor issues, then let out again."

"What does that do?"

"Makes them not want to do it again?"

"Seems oversimplified."

Rock *hmmpfed*, then turned her attention to peering down the corridor. "Can we concentrate?"

"Oh, right."

It wasn't too hard to stay out of sight in a place where pyrsi were confined into side rooms, and the corridors were only sporadically patrolled. At least, not for the old team of Rock and Dime, she thought with amusement and a lingering pang of fondness.

It was also fairly easy to follow the structure of the passageways themselves. There seemed to be a main corridor leading away from the cells, barren and covered in splotches of dark color, and dotted with charged glowstones. A few corridors branched out to where Rock said the main prison was, and soon the corridor turned back, to what Dime thought was deeper into the cliff. After one steep curve, they almost walked right into a guard. *A High Guard.*

Dime tried not to gasp when she saw xyr distinctive diamond pin. She hoped, desperately hoped, xe was not part of Neimano's group. She'd hoped Neimano's guards were out scanning Ada-ji for her, not looking here. Part of her gamble was that they didn't think she'd come back. Not so soon, at least. Neimano clearly liked to plot. She'd hoped he was still plotting.

Not willing to lose the chance now, Dime marched up to the guard as if xe reported to her. "Hello, there. No escort is required. Thank you." By xyr reaction, she had the impression standing guard at this spot was a tradition or formality, as Ella had indicated the idea of coming here without permission would be unthinkable to a Fo-ror. Xyr eyes wide, the High Guard looked positively surprised to see anyone, let alone a pair of Ja-lal.

"I can't let you back here," xe said. "Are you really—"

"You haven't heard? *Hmm.* I'm not authorized to tell you anything, of course. Here, maybe this will clarify." Dime reached into her bag. Nervous about too much fumbling around, she was relieved when her fingers fell on a smooth shape. She was taking a gamble on this one.

She held out the engraved pen that Ferala had used, by valence, to write the note on Tikinal's paper. When she'd seen the accents of gold over the elaborately engraved wood, she'd asked for it, on a hunch. In a short time, she'd seen how much both rank and symbolism meant to the elite here.

Sure enough, once she'd sat, resting on a cliff ledge, she'd taken it out to find a twirling *F* inscribed into what looked like high-grade, genuine gold. It made sense that Ferala had sent his own pen over by valence to scribble the quick note, rather than manipulate one of his clerk's. Consent aside, pyrsi did like using their own pens. She showed the *F* to the guard, who stood taller in response.

"There?" She peered right into xyr face, flicking the pen back. "I was told I could use this. I don't think he'd want attention drawn to my presence here, wouldn't you agree?"

"Burge," xe said the word hesitantly as though not sure how to address a Ja-lal, "I'm sure that he wouldn't."

"Good," Dime put the pen back into her bag. "If he asks if we arrived safely, in private of course, please tell him that we did. Otherwise, best not to speak of our mission."

"Of course, Burgess." The guard curved his fingers the same way Volana had in the forest. Dime returned the gesture.

"Ambassador, with me." Dime nodded to Rock.

Rock returned a curt nod and followed closely behind as they walked through the huge door. It closed behind them. "You've become creative with words."

"Hey." Dime had thought through this carefully. "I've said nothing untrue to anyone." Rock *did* always choose Ambassador when they played realms. "At worst case, I'm exploiting pyrsi's assumptions. And maybe those assumptions need a challenge or two."

Ends didn't justify means, but Dime had thought a lot lately about the damage caused by the hard lines pyrsi drew. She didn't need to draw her own to counter them, as long as she was comfortable with her actions. And she wasn't going to be lectured by Rock, a pyr who didn't even have *tattoos*. How was that not just as sketchy?

Rock grunted. "Either way, let's get some distance before he does his considering," she whispered, pulling a glowstone out of her own bag. "*Ambassador.* Ridiculous. Let's go."

Dime agreed with that. Rock raised the glowstone, and Dime

tripped in surprise, grabbing Rock's arm as she extended it to her. Dime let go.

Around them, the stone's light shone on walls filled with small chunks of crystal, perfectly refracting the light as it hit them.

"Holy. Sol." Rock gripped the light tighter.

"Distance?" Dime reminded, trying to pretend she wasn't stunned herself.

Rock nodded, her mouth still open.

They stepped into the room, and Dime got out a notebook, drawing quick but clear maps as they walked. Many of the caves were bare, some merely corridors. Every once in a while, they'd widen to a larger space, covered again in the shining crystals. Many of the passages wound upward, others down. Knowing how downhill slopes could trap climbers, and nervous from the echoes of trickling water, they kept mostly to the upward forks.

As they progressed inward, Dime recognized a feeling here, the itch she'd felt from being in the prisons, but now opened to more of a gentle burn. So it had been the diamonds she'd felt before. Maybe all Fo-ror felt them. Maybe the smaller uses of valences in the complex served also as a release, being so close to such potential for more.

The further into the caves they climbed, the crystals set into the wall grew larger and more prevalent. They wound back for quite a while, both through the diamond-lined caves and plainer, winding passages. Dime continued to push forward, hoping the further they went, the harder they'd be to find. Just in case. They turned, walking into a particularly large room.

Exhaling with a weird balloonish noise, Rock plopped onto the floor. "This is enough. If they find us back here, they deserve to."

Dime hoped the High Guard wouldn't mention them. Or even if he grew suspicious, he'd not want to offer that he'd let them in, maybe worried he'd reveal a secret of Ferala's. And, she hoped, when Rock was discovered missing, they'd assume she'd left.

If by any chance the two events were connected, Dime didn't know whether they'd send pyrsi in to search or just wait for them to emerge. But she was really here—it was hard to believe—and she wasn't leaving until she was ready. She turned to see Rock staring at her.

"The diamond mines. Impressive. So, uh, what's the plan?"

"So, it turns out that valence doesn't come from wings."

"It comes from diamonds?"

"No, diamonds just make it easier. It comes from,"—she wanted to say *the heart* but stopped—"inside."

"Then why do Fo-ror have it and not Ja-lal?"

"It has to do with their wings."

"You just said—"

"Ok, not the flying part of the wings. But it comes from a tissue that grows from the heart into the wings. And maybe I still have some of that tissue inside."

"Wait. You're not just a fairy. You're a caster fairy? With a . . . wing stub?"

She let that pass. "I think so. We're here to find out."

Rock shook her head. "And we couldn't have done this, like, out at a den? Or some isolated forest cabin? I heard they have nice ones out by a big lake."

Dime bristled at the mention of the lake; she knew that was Home Sha to the Newts, the one they'd been driven from for the Fo-ror's convenience. "We could have. But Ella thought it'd be dangerous. And we might draw the Fo-ror Seats right to us."

"As opposed to here, in their actual caves."

"Yes. First, the diamonds here should amplify any power, so I shouldn't need to have a fit of rage, meaning I hopefully won't rend the land."

"I feel like there's more you haven't told me," Rock muttered.

Dime continued, talking over her. "Second, the diamonds should shield anyone outside from sensing the use of valence here. As opposed to zapping it out in some random piece of the plains and then being caught. So that's the theory."

"What about that one you wear?"

Dime pulled the pendant out, and even here, surrounded by crystals much larger, it stood out, with its soft geometric shape and a faint blue glow. "This one's unique." She felt practically parental saying this when surrounded by hundreds like it, especially as Ella had insisted it was rare. But that wasn't the point at the moment, so she continued on. "Apparently I've stored more than two epochs of angst into it. You know, charged and tuned like the diamond keys are, just . . . monumental."

"Can anyone else use it?" Rock blinked. "I mean, other fairies? Or is it tuned, like the key? Except, you could use the key?" She stared off at the wall, biting her lip.

"I think I re-tuned the key. And it didn't require much charge; it was just a little chip and Waynium was only a little angsty. From what I understand, which is very little, this pendant is only tuned to me. It could be used by someone else or charged over time, but whatever valence I've placed in it could only be used by me."

"Harm, D."

"Yeah, I know." Unease crept over her, like the nerves that set in right before asking someone out, or before finding out whether she'd been accepted to something competitive that she really wanted to do.

"So, you dragged me back here. Are you, uh, going to do some valence?"

The mention of valence jarred Dime from her anxiety. She stared at Rock, working through what she'd said. "Oh. Yes. We should get to that." Dime set down her bag.

Interlude

The time of Sol's rise shifted just a little each turn, and Ran had learned to sense it, since he couldn't keep to the bells this far from the city. He treasured these moments, when the darkness turned to light. He tried not to miss a single one.

That wasn't so hard out here, up in the norwes. He missed his friends in the city at times, but they all had their own lives. And he had his.

He'd built a rocking chair on the porch that faced Sol's rise. He'd always wanted a chair and a porch, and nothing else on his mind, and he'd worked long cycles in the district to get here. Content, he wandered to his porch, staring out into the rich blackness that was the night. The rocking chair tilted as he sat back.

Hints of deep color feathered the mountains—plum, mauve, and deep iridescent shades almost indistinguishable from the night itself. He ran his hands around the glass of citrused water that he held, too brisk to sample just yet.

In a single instant, the first rays of brightness jumped over the mountains. Like watercolor paint absorbing into canvas, strokes of golden mustard leaked over the edges of the land, topped with the juice of red fruits, highlighting each bump and peak of the hills beyond. The burst of light cut a bite from the mountain, just in the spot where it emerged, framed with the dusky pink of a mountain rose.

A flash of brightness pierced his view, as a white star emerged and disappeared, flaring into a great ball of brightness and spirit. Above, the sky's plum hues had softened into a sweet blue, and Sol rose through its clouds like a mythical diamond.

The glow atop the mountain ridges faded into peach, and bright rays streamed onto his porch until only a muted silver provided the canvas for the rolling clouds above. Ran tightened his grip against the glass of tart water and took a long, invigorating drink.

"Good morning," he said to Ada-ji, starting to get up from his seat.

Instead, he sat back down again.

Act 2

CRYSTALS

"**I have no idea** what I'm supposed to do." Dime wiggled her fingers in the air.

"This light is getting dim. You could start there." By the nervous look on Rock's face, the idea of plunging into darkness was distressing. See, and here Dime thought the IC agent wasn't scared of anything. Dime was scared of all of it.

"Do you want to set it down, first?" Dime asked, glancing nervously at the weakening glowstone in Rock's hand.

Rock shook her head and held the stone up. Unknown effects of fairy powers aside, the stone was heavy, and Dime didn't know what could happen. Oh, Rock could take care of herself.

Either way, Dime had zero idea how to begin filling a stone with light. How to change the world around her without her own direct touch. Except, she'd done it before, so she could do it again. Trying to focus, she remembered the concepts Ella had discussed.

First, valence came from the heart. So, she needed to pull from herself, not from the object. Second, the diamonds surrounding her should magnify any energy she released, and by the size and number of diamonds in this cave alone, that had to be an understatement. She could feel them around her, bolstering her with an almost physical effect. Her sense grew clear why she needed to try as little as possible, easing into it.

Into what? She still didn't know what to *do*. Wasn't this why fairies had trainers? How was she supposed to jump into this now, midway through life? With nothing. Maybe this was too much.

No. She didn't come this far not to give it a go.

Dime tried to clear her mind. She saw Rock's worried face. She set it aside. She saw the softly glowing stone. It needed energy, to provide light. Nothing more. The diamonds surrounded her. She felt her heart beating, and the diamond pendant, resting above it. She thought about her father, naming her for the pendant. His smile, and his songs. She loved him so much.

The stone needed light. Dime could give it light. She reached her fingers out, and willed that the stone *would have light.*

Rock squealed as the stone flew from her hand and exploded in a bright flash, as they threw their arms over their faces to shield them from the shower of little fragments of stone hitting and rolling across the cave floor.

"Maybe that was too much," Dime said, as they sat in complete darkness. Her heart thumped in her chest.

"Maybe I shouldn't hold it next time," Rock added, her breaths sharp.

In the distance, a pounding noise emerged. It was muffled, as if very far away or within the rock itself. They both held silent.

"What was that?" Rock finally asked. "You didn't do that, right?"

"No, I didn't. And I don't know. Are you ok?"

"I might have peed a little."

The rumbles stopped.

"Dime. It's really dark in here." Rock sounded upset.

With the light gone, Dime instead tried to sense the room around her. Maybe like driving a toothcar, the surroundings were more important than the road.

With the diamonds resonating around her, more than just sound and smell emerged; she didn't know if she was sensing the room or imagining it—diamonds, stone, entrances to other chambers. Passages of unknown depth and reach. The breathing of the cave itself, little cracks and tunnels bringing fresh air from the surface. The fragments of the glowstone, mixed in with the dusty gravel. The top of the cave, and the layers of stone above. The depth of Ada-ji, below. The Sol that warmed it and the cool Sha against which it rested.

The more she concentrated, the more the world came into her consciousness, expanding around her, with no known boundary. Dime stood in the middle of all this, small, but possessing her own energy. Her own ability to impact.

An energy flowed between her and Rock, calming her. She could hear Rock's breaths, rapid in the pitch dark. She started to imagine light flowing into the rocks, but stopped. *Too much, remember?*

Instead of thinking about the stones, she concentrated on the idea of light. The room, alight. Started by a tiny speck, one fully within her control. So small it could rest in her hand. Even smaller. She didn't need to be all-powerful. She just needed to be enough.

The ceiling burst into light, flooding the room as in broad daylight. Around them, the diamonds glimmered and reflected, with rainbows jumping in and out. Dime lowered her hands, which she realized she'd been extending.

"How did you do that?" Rock blinked, the brightness illuminating her tightly shaven head, wide eyes, and blue lips.

"I thought about change. How things were now, and how I wanted them to be. And I made a connection between the two."

"Such power," Rock whispered.

She felt fraudulent, for she'd just sort of zoned out and then in, and then realized she'd done something. But that shouldn't matter; the results were the point, not her. Clearing her mind of guilt or doubt, she continued. "I also tried not to force it. I accepted that I was small, but still enough to help. In this vision of light, I focused on a single spark, not needing to know exactly where my one spark led to know I was contributing. It was less intimidating that way. Something I thought I could do—which made me believe that I could."

"Could you put the lamp stone back together?" Rock shielded her eyes a little. "I mean, the original one."

Dime shook her head. "It doesn't feel right. Parts of that stone are mixed in with other pieces of the cave now. What happened has happened. No. I can't explain it fully, but I don't want to try that."

"Then turn this down, maybe?"

Dime swept her hand, and drew back some of the light. The room returned to a pleasant glow. She stared at her fingers, realizing how easily she'd just done that.

Her nerves were turning quickly to excitement. She reached into her backpack and pulled out a handful of castanuts, setting all but one onto the floor. Nestling a single castanut in her palm, she looked to a natural ledge on the far side of the room.

She wanted the nut on the ledge. Imagining only the faintest idea of motion, she considered the path for the nut to be on the ledge, and she told the nut to move toward the ledge.

It stayed in her hand.

Trying again, she considered motion, and what it would take for the nut to rest on that ledge. She imagined it.

The nut flew from her hand, shattering against the sparkling diamond wall.

"Harm's way," Rock muttered.

"Rock, I said this might be dangerous. I don't want you to be in any danger. If you want to wait in another room—"

"Do you want me to go to another room?"

"No," she answered, honestly. "It sort of . . . calms me, with you here." That came out more directly than Dime had intended it, but Rock only settled back against the wall and started rummaging into Dime's bag. Well, she did like having her here. And they'd agreed to be friends, so.

Fine, it was more than that. An old fondness. She was just glad she was here. Dime picked up the next castanut and rolled it in her fingers.

Of the next dozen or so nuts, only two more exploded against the wall. Some rolled down into a crevice and others bounced and cracked. None found their way to the ledge. For all Dime's theories, there seemed to be more art to valence than logic.

"You're trying too hard."

"What?" Dime looked over at Rock, who had found Dime's stash of fruit sticks and was helping herself.

"When you turned the light on, it was because you needed to. Not because you forced it. Do you need to put that on the ledge?"

"No." She looked at the nut in her hands.

"So that's your problem."

But that didn't make sense. The fairies used valence almost exclusively now, from what she'd seen, for trivial things. They didn't need to lift plates and cups. They just wanted to. It wasn't that simple. Still, what Rock had said about forcing—maybe that was a good point.

Dime closed her eyes. The nut could be on the ledge; she believed it. She stopped worrying about it and felt the diamonds around her, and the path the nut would take. The nut danced in her imagination, cradled to its location.

She opened her eyes. Her hand was empty in front of her, and a brown, plump castanut rocked back and forth on the narrow ledge.

"See," Rock said, leaning back. Dime almost hissed.

Four more nuts joined the first. Inside, she expected to feel some warmth or power, but she was calm. In fact, calmer than she'd been in as long as she could remember. Only a small energy crackled inside, felt in her center back and the very edges of her fingertips.

She'd spilled a lot of nuts in her earlier efforts, and Dime didn't want to leave a mess. She could clean this place up.

Whoosh.

All the shards of nuts zoomed together into a pile onto the ledge. One too many joined in, and one of the whole nuts wavered, before falling off. It cracked against the floor. Her fingers felt a hint of fatigue. She flexed them.

"D. Explain to me again why you didn't just do this earlier? I mean, not now, but in your life. Wouldn't there have been some big incident as a ch'pyr or something? I mean, not with nuts. But, you know, like a window broke and you were like 'oh no!' and repaired it?"

That had been on Dime's mind a lot since Lodon. She was probably very fortunate something of that nature hadn't happened. Yes, she'd had to unknowingly carry the burden longer, but she might not have been ready, earlier, to handle it. Who knew? Honestly, she was tired of worrying about moot points. But she did have an answer for Rock.

"I didn't use it before because I didn't know that I could. I often told my team that sometimes someone needs to tell you what you can do, if you don't see it yourself. Maybe that applies here."

Suddenly, the fact that she was using valence overwhelmed her. The new calm she felt, and the sparkle of the diamonds, and all the potential she might hold. "All these diamonds. My diamond. I feel like I could do anything in here."

"Then do anything."

Sometimes, Rock was a little much. Dime forgot that they were older now, and a quick memory of her and Rock together pulled her backward to cycles long past. Young and unsettled, they'd found each other in the eye of the same storm, and she knew, even if she hadn't admitted it before, there was a bond between them that had never weakened. It would have to be different, now, but with her heightened senses, it surrounded her.

Rock didn't seem affected, or uneasy. She seemed fine. She was willing to be friends. She was just sitting there, going through another of Dime's snacks. How many had she eaten? That was annoying.

Rock could stop pilfering my snacks.

The fruit stick lifted into the air, spinning around. Dime panicked, feeling guilty for the petty act. The stick tumbled to the ground, where Rock reached over and flipped it into her hand. She brushed it off with the other and took another bite.

"D?"

"I'm sorry. I just—"

"Did it help? Are you there now?"

"I don't know. Maybe?" Tired and confused, Dime walked over and sat next to Rock. They sat a long time, Dime deep in thought.

She watched the light bouncing off the crystals, and she knew it could be even more dazzling. Not worried about something as innocent as pure light, she divided it with her fingers, and separated it into beams and angles, and before she understood it, the room was filled with wide, dazzling rainbows, shining brightly against each wall.

Rock lifted her hand into the air, and bright blue spread across her palm.

"*Ooooh*," she marveled. "You're getting it."

Realizing what she'd done, Dime stopped. She didn't understand how she stopped it, but she stopped it anyway. She *felt* it now. The large rainbows disappeared, leaving the smaller ones, glimmering as they faded away. It felt so natural, not even in her fingers, but in her senses. No. This was worse. This *scared* her.

"What?" Rock asked.

Dime gathered the courage to answer. "I'm scared I could hurt pyrsi," she eeked out. The long silence worried her. But she didn't know what else to say.

After a while, Rock leaned forward. "What if you could help them? Would that be worth it?"

"I don't know," Dime answered. What was she here for? Had she hoped it wouldn't work after all? Well. It did. "Rock? You're really good at plans and . . . consequences. So I'm trying to help us—protect us from, war, I guess? What should I be practicing?"

"You mean, what do you need to prevent a war? Sol, D, how do I answer that? Don't you think if single pyrsi could have prevented wars, there'd never have been one?"

Then what was Dime doing here? Was it just to learn to control herself, or was it to try something bigger? It was so frustrating to be pulled out of her life and not know how she could return to it—to continue to take huge risks without a clear vision of the outcome. Yet, there was no alternative. She couldn't pretend that things would just go back to how they were. Or that they should.

Those turns had passed.

"So, valence, it does more than just throw nuts and take my snacks, right?" Rock shifted from her cross-legged seat, raising her knees in front of her.

"What are you talking about?"

"We've just been fearing the fairies forever, right? I'll be a little underwhelmed if the best you've got for me is levitating a nut and sweeping the floor. Though, the rainbows were nice."

Harm it, Rock, that's what I've been saying. "Well, what am I supposed to do with it?"

"Am I the fairy here?"

Dime growled, as in literally, and thought about what she would do with the valence if she could. She'd help pyrsi. Ok. What did that mean? She'd help heal the sick and injured, except she didn't think she could use valence that way. Ella said it impacted objects around her. Like, how she'd made a toothcar drive on its own.

It seemed obvious that if one had broad powers, one would immediately work off a list of wrongs to be righted. She'd erase hemsas and protect pyrsi from the ill-intentioned or ill-founded. She'd provide resources, repair structures, and spread joy. She'd provide a platform for issues to be heard, and artists to be seen. She'd help pyrsi to love, more than judge. Here, in a sparkly cave and under Rock's skeptical eyes, she was left just . . . staring at her fingers.

She thought back to the spark of light. Maybe she couldn't change the world tonight. Maybe she just needed to believe that she could help.

A small harmonica Dayn had bought in the village flew from her bag, and she shot the air through it. It honked like a bird, but it played, as breeze circled in the cave. The freeform music felt joyful, and it prompted her to make even more. Two pencils flew out, and the notebook where they'd drawn the map. The pencils began to strum an uneven beat on the binding, giving a loose frame to the wheezy music. The broken pieces of castanut jumped up and down, like a shaker, filling in a syncopated rhythm.

Rock started to laugh. Not a teasing laugh, but a genuine one. Distracted, Dime smiled at her and the objects tumbled to the ground.

If stones could glow, then light could dance. She remembered what Seat Dailawe had done back in the prison. Dime knew that was possible, since she'd seen it. Sparkles, then. Dime flung her fingers, and blue sparks popped in the air. First one, then three, then ten. Then the room was filled with sparks. Dime danced in a circle as they fizzled out.

Finally, she sat down, across from Rock. "I feel it now. I feel how it works. Except, I'm sorry, we talked about how to prevent a war, and that was all frivolous."

Rock started to answer, but the rumbling sounded again, interrupting her. Dust released from the ceiling, raining down on them. Dime and Rock stuck their faces into their sleeves.

"This place has been here since all time, right? Is there a reason it's falling apart while we're in it?"

Dime was starting to recognize the energy in herself. The valence. It was indeed a signature, as part of her as her heart itself. There was no way she was causing the rumbling. She would know. It felt distant, as if far into the caves. Dime didn't know how far the caves extended, or how many of them held diamonds. The caves ran under the Great Cliff, which meant they were actually underneath Sol's Reach, even now.

It struck her.

"It's us!" She snapped around to face Rock. "No, not you and I. It's the Circles. The Construction Circle, and their Boring Project. They're on the plains digging. Are they trying to find this place?" The sounds rumbled from a distance.

"What?"

"The plains are above us. There were boring machines there; I remember it now. The Construction Circle. What else would they be digging for, out so far?"

Rock's face turned sour. "Are you serious? No contact with the fairies or the Violence will return, except let's ram a drill down into their sacred space and hope that goes fine? What are they doing? *Does Sala know?*"

Dime glared up at the ceiling, as if she could see Ada-ji's plains, stretching out above her and to the nor. She remembered the large machine she'd seen, the maps back in Lodon. Eclipsing the barely conscious touch that had played the music and lit the sparks, anger burst from her fingers, shooting upward. A spike of stone shook loose, and Dime started as—

Rock slammed into her, pushing her out of its path.

On top of Dime now, Rock held her face tight, grimacing in pain.

Dime wriggled out from under her and winced at the pool of blood seeping through Rock's shirt. "Stay still! Don't move. Don't move. Let me look!" She pulled the shirt up and yanked it off.

"Oh! I'm sorry!" Dime was horrified she hadn't asked first. Rock was conscious and fully able to consent. It's just, she'd seen the injury, and it was like those turns when they'd been familiar.

"It's fine. It's fine. Do whatever you need. How bad is it? *Harmbird*, that hurts!"

A stone flew into Dime's hand, lighting up with bright, white light. The spike that had fallen lay next to them, bloodless itself, but with a razor-sharp edge from where it had split from the cave's ceiling. The skin of Rock's upper back was sliced as cleanly, but it had pulled wide open, just under the shoulder blade, tissues visible from within. Dime reeled at the severity of the wound.

Rock was losing too much blood. Several thoughts spun past. She should get a thread and needle and try to sew it closed; she had those in her bag. She might not have time—Rock was bleeding too fast. Dime could wrench closed the skin with her hands, and try and hold it, but for how long? Was anything damaged inside that would harm her if treated by a simple surface repair? Could Dime use her valence, to move the blood back into her body or to press the skin? No, the gathered blood would be dirty. Dime had no medical training. Could she command the bleeding to stop?

A streak of color caught her eye. In the deepness of the cut, and through the dark blood, the light caught a tissue and glimmered back. Purples, blues, iridescent. Unmistakable. This was something she'd have to think about when she had time. No time, now. Her mind raced, but she knew it. It made sense.

"Rock. Listen to me. I'm afraid to mess you up worse. I think that ... Ja-lal might have valence too. I know that's a lot. I need you to trust me. Just, do what I was doing. You don't have the tuned pendant, but there are diamonds all around us. Let them help. Know that it is possible to heal. Believe it is possible. Don't force it, just imagine your tissues fusing back together and channel yourself into that belief. Fix the cut. Please. It's bad. If you can, I mean. I don't know how to fix it. You have to try."

Rock's breathing was rapid, and she wasn't answering. Dime had done this. This was Dime's fault. Rock had saved her, been her strength here. She couldn't lose her. Rock didn't deserve this.

"Rock, I need you to trust me. Please. I need you."

At first, Dime thought maybe she'd done something, but she felt nothing in her fingers, and as she moved them away, she saw that Rock's skin was changing, like tiny waves were passing through it. As they passed, the layers were drawing closer. "You're doing it," she whispered.

As fascinated as she was terrified, Dime watched the tissues work and change and rejoin, until the wound was closed, replaced by a slick of blood over unbroken skin. Her hands shaking, she found her flask, pouring water over Rock's shoulder and back. Only an uneven, blurred line remained where the cut had been.

With that, Dime was done using valence. She was not going to hurt anyone again. She'd seen how it worked, she knew how to control it, and now she could push it back inside herself, where it had been before—and she was *never* using it again. She handed Rock her crumpled blue shirt and didn't even consider whether valence could repair it.

"Let's go."

Rock held the shirt in her hand, staring ahead.

"We've got to go. Don't you get it? I hurt you. I did that. Not the Circles. I got pissed off at them and wanted to break their machines. I wanted to commit the Violence against their drills. I wanted that. And some of those thoughts sprayed out and I almost killed you. Great friend, I am. I'm sorry. Let's go."

Rock finally looked up. "D, stop. Please. Stop. We'll talk about it. But did you just say Ja-lal have valence, and did I just heal myself with it?"

First, she'd hurt her friend, and now she was being selfish. Great. Dime didn't even know how to be surprised anymore, so she tried to understand what a shock this must all be to Rock. All she could see was that wound, sliced open, the image flashing in her mind. She'd done that. She'd hurt her. "It doesn't matter. We're not using it again. I understand, now, why Ella needed me to see for myself. Valence cannot be used. That's the key to all this. I've solved it."

A grimace replaced Rock's dazed expression, and her eyes became alert again. "No, no, no," she repeated, pulling on her shirt. "Ooh, a little breezy in back. You are not giving up now. We had a setback. That happens. It always happens. You don't give up the first time something goes wrong."

"A setback? I attacked you! With the Violence!"

"You did?"

No, of course she hadn't meant to attack Rock. Yet her anger and carelessness had done it anyway. Rock had almost *died*.

"Can we at least talk about it first?" Rock offered, pulling herself to a seat.

Still shaking, Dime supposed she owed Rock whatever she wanted at this point. "Briefly," she agreed, feeling a coldness from the room around her.

Rock snorted. "Fine, briefly. Answer me. What was the difference? Between the blue sparks and what happened after?"

Hadn't she told her? Why was she making her say it again? "I told you. I was mad. I was angry, realizing how the Ja-lal were endangering the Fo-ror, reinforcing all their claims that we're dangerous brutes. And after epochs of being told the Fo-ror were the problem too, well, maybe we're the harmed problem. Who knows, maybe we caused the killed-off curse too. Maybe it's always been us."

Rock was waiting, as if she hadn't answered the question.

"Ok. Fine. The way I got it to work earlier was by envisioning change, envisioning a state of how things could be. Instead of creating that future, I was angry at the present and wanted to stop it, without worrying about how."

Rock leaned forward. "You could say the first creates paths. The second creates walls."

"I suppose you could say that." Dime wasn't feeling so poetic about it. They should leave.

"So, then, you can't stop practicing. You need to learn the difference. Ella said you have the powerful diamond, right? And all those cycles of channeling, right? You've been given that power, whether you wanted it or not. And you're going to use it. It's going to come bursting out of you. It already has. I know you, D. If you don't accept who you are, you're going to stay pissed off, and then pyrsi might get hurt."

"I could throw the diamond out. Right here."

"You could," Rock agreed. "Who would that help? Less power on the side of peace? Is that what you want? The diamond doesn't hurt pyrsi, D."

No, I do.

And that cut to the heart of what had been tripping her ever since she learned that her pendant empowered valence. It wasn't whether she deserved the diamond or not. She didn't. It was the unknown of who had given it to her. What they wanted her to do with it. And whether holding onto the potential power to help pyrsi really justified holding onto the potential power to harm them.

No one needed a diamond to hurt pyrsi. Rock had that right. But it made it easier, and maybe some things weren't meant to be easier.

"I know," she said, feeling too tired and sad and overwhelmed to parse this all out right now.

"Just don't make any big decisions yet. Right after a traumatic event is the worst time to make decisions. It's a time to reflect, but not to decide. And this 'curse'—causing a disease to kill Fo-ror? No Ja-lal would do such a thing. No *pyr* would do such a thing."

"Nar burned down that house." She shouldn't have brought that up, judging by the pain that flashed across Rock's face. Their eyes met.

"Keep it for now. Please?" Rock didn't argue the rest, Dime noted.

Reluctantly, she didn't throw her crystal into the cave. She did push it back under her shirt. "Let's leave. I understand how it works now. I have the sense of valence and plenty to think about and practice, if I decide to. I don't want to stay here. There's too much power."

"Hey, it's not like I don't know that," Rock snapped. "Harm. I'm sorry. I'm not trying to be all Solshine either. Just don't abandon everything you've gained here so quickly. Trust me?"

Dime glanced over, touched by the sincerity in Rock's expression and so, so grateful her friend was ok. "Maybe I can stop it," she mused. "Nothing burst out of me before. Maybe it won't again now that I understand it."

Rock *tsked*. "You know it doesn't work that way. You don't forget your experiences. It didn't burst out before because you didn't think it was possible before."

"No, I made the toothcar move. I realize that now. When I was driving across Sol's Reach and I'd practically collapsed, valence was propelling the car forward. I could have saved my knee joints some wear by taking my feet off the pedals."

"You'd just seen the fairies then. Something you thought wasn't real. Then they were real. New possibilities. Besides, Dime, you had wings too. No matter how long ago, maybe your body remembered that, even if you didn't. It saw the wings and was like, hallo!"

"My body doesn't say 'hallo.'"

Rock leaned back, wincing a little. "You're just trying to argue with me."

"Are you alright?" Dime could tell Rock was still in pain.

"Back's still sore. Maybe I did it wrong. So, how did you know I could do that? And we're not done about your quitting yet, but we're hiding the banner a bit. *Ja-lal have valence?*" Rock opened her hands to her sides.

"I know. I'd just gotten used to the idea I may have valence. Now, everyone?" Her head was starting to ache. "I can harm pyrsi. I don't want to. I go to the caves. Ja-lal are trying to crush the caves, or something. Ja-lal have valence." *I hurt my friend.* She looked at Rock, slumping her head to the side. "Can life just go back to normal?"

"Sure," Rock grinned. "We'll just reestablish normal. This is it!" She stood, brushing off her pants, apparently indicating her concession to leave.

Dime's mind felt so cluttered. She rested her temples into her hands, trying to ignore that the white hair had to be almost visible by now. Rock was definitely going to notice.

"D, if you're worried about your ominous power, remember you're much, much more powerful here. Right?"

That was true. "Being here is overwhelming. I don't like it, not at all. I feel too powerful. It's too . . . disproportionate. Not everyone can be in here. So, who gets let in? Who should?"

"So you'd close the whole place down. Seems like a waste."

She wasn't going to argue this right now. She rose, just glad they were leaving. "I don't know." Of all the competing thoughts racing in her mind, one floated to the surface. That stone was going to cut *her*, not Rock. Rock had pushed her out of the way. *Ah, Sol.* "Hey. Thank you for saving me. I'm sorry you got hurt. I feel horrible about it."

"Of course you do. I didn't want to get hurt either. I was too slow."

"Rock."

"I know."

"I've missed you, all these cycles," Dime blurted. "Even when I didn't think about it, it's like you said with the wings. Something was there, remembering. I'm glad to see you again. I know it's not like before, but I'm glad we can be friends."

Rock turned away. Dime didn't mean to sound so forward, but she felt groggy and she was sorting through a lot. Ja-lal valence. What did that *mean*? And, she supposed, wings grew inside? But there were medics. Surgery had been done on Ja-lal time and time again; surely someone had noticed.

Of course, if you'd never seen a wing, you wouldn't know what looked like one.

The caves rumbled again. Distracted from whatever she'd been thinking, she held still, feeling the sounds and vibrations from the distance. This time, she tried to hold calm. "The Fo-ror have to know this is going on. The Seats, specifically. They have to know."

Rock only nodded.

"These caves aren't the only place at risk," Dime continued. Her father had often told her about the water system of Lodon, so she knew how critical its design and maintenance were. The water that flowed past Lodon and down into the gorge must make its way to the Heartland underground, through the Great Cliff.

"If we caused a disruption of the cave system, the water that flows through Pito might be affected. Waterflow to the whole forest, maybe. And more directly—how much of Pito would be crushed in a collapse of the Great Cliff? Would it kill the Seats? The workers? Would it rumble out into the city, killing thousands? And why is it up to us to stop any of this?" Again, she urgently tried to calm herself.

Rock tapped her hands together before speaking. "I guess my answer to that is because we know about it." She glanced aside. "And since we can."

Dime's panic was mounting. "Let's get out of here. Let's go. I promise I'll keep the necklace for now. I'll think about everything. Let's get home."

"Honestly, D? This is not my favorite place. I support this decision."

"All these diamonds." Dime suddenly realized that unlike when she'd performed valence peacefully, the accident with Rock had clouded her mind again, like the incident with the Sol's Pillars when she'd left Lodon. Not as severely, but she didn't feel right. She tried to gather herself, taking long, slow breaths. "All these diamonds."

"And the thought doesn't even cross your mind to take some back to the city."

"No. It doesn't. What we need now isn't more power." Dime remembered what Volana had said. "It's more . . . voice."

Rock tilted her head. "Ok. So, how are we going to get out of here?"

Dime knew *here* meant the complex, not just the caves. And she'd thought about this one, at least. "I was careful getting in, because there were things I needed. I needed to find you, uninterrupted. I needed to make sure you were free. I needed to get into the caves and spend some time, uninterrupted. Now, I just need to leave. And it's funny—I was in the same situation at the complex."

"Our complex? The Circles?"

"Oh, I didn't tell you? I snuck into the IC and got some info I needed."

Rock stepped back, grinning. "You, sneaking in there! I love it. You should have made a den to watch *them*. Took some reports on them!"

Dime wasn't going to tell Rock about the sandwich banners. There were limits.

"Info, though?" Rock asked. "What info did you need? There's no info on this place, not that you'd have access to."

Dime remembered that Rock was part of a secret shadow Circle, one that gathered information on the Fo-ror, their goal being a careful watch to prevent the return of the Violence or anything that could lead to another Great War. Rock had also told her that they frequently planted ideas in small, subtle ways, not enough to draw the attention of the known Circles, but enough to calm suspicion and fear. Enough to place doubt between fear and action.

"I picked up a map." She knew Rock wasn't going to buy that she'd gone all the way to records just for a map. "And also . . . there were others like me."

Rock exhaled.

"Yes. Exactly. I didn't want to invade their privacy, but I felt obligated to warn them. I only found two. Please, don't tell anyone else. It's not their business."

"I won't. And I didn't mean to pry. So, what were you saying, about getting out?"

"Oh. Well, when I left the complex," she said, trying to brighten her tone, "I just left. They all saw me. Was tired of hiding, anyway. Tired of it here."

"So that's why you walked into this place in a lampshade."

"Well, I'm never doing it again. I swore, and swore, and I'm *serious* this time. I just needed everyone safe first. The minute we walk through that door, I am going to be Dime every lasting moment of my life. No matter what."

"If that's what you needed to find here, I'm glad you found it," Rock said, picking up her bag.

It's not that— Oh, whatever. Dime stood and cinched her bag back up onto her shoulders. "Here, let me carry yours." She wasn't sure how sore Rock's shoulder was.

"I'm fine. I'd tell you to zap it lighter, but I don't want anything else falling on me."

"That's not funny!" It really wasn't.

Rock hopped over the gravelly part and picked up one of the stone fragments that had fallen from the ceiling, still glowing with light. Together, they wound again through the caves, checking their hand-drawn map at each turn. As they'd mostly gone uphill before, they now moved mostly downward.

Since they were leaving, Dime gave herself permission to marvel at the beauty of the diamonds as they hiked, without worrying about their significance. She wasn't sure she'd ever see them again. Or that she'd want to.

Finally, they arrived back at the entrance, where the large, heavy door remained shut. Rock set the glowstone down on the floor, where it cast an eerie spotlight against the door's worn carvings.

Dime was nervous as to whether the guard would still be waiting on the other side, but she saw no way out except through the door, so she pushed it open. She *did* use a little bit of valence as she couldn't quite push it without. Rock didn't need to know that.

To her surprise, the doorway was empty.

"Where'd the guard go?" Dime wondered aloud.

"Maybe he realized we weren't supposed to be back there?"

"Then why aren't they here to meet us?"

They didn't need to figure out what the guards did or didn't know at this point. They just needed to get out.

As they hurried through the long corridors past what Dime now understood was both the prison and the dead caves—dead of diamonds, she supposed—they met no one and heard no one. Near the front area lined with cages, the sounds of a commotion emerged. Arguing voices rang down the corridor.

"Maybe they're arguing over the birds?" Rock offered. "They were sort of a hot topic in the complex, at least from the number of 'I'm not here, but . . .' visits I got over them." Rock was trying to joke, but Dime had seen in her expression the urgency of not being recaptured. Should they just run past?

Dime thought a moment. "Would you work in a place with only one exit?"

"I would not. Let's go."

Turning on their heels, they hurried now a new direction, turning each corner with occasional arguing over which way would lead back to the outer complex. They almost ran past a big, heavy door, without a doorknob, like the ones Dime had seen around the

Seats' private rooms. "Stop," Dime whispered. "Look!" She swung it open and they stepped through, Rock staying close.

Back in the corridors of the Seats' complex, they were all at once surrounded by winged pyrsi, gasping and dropping their books at the sight of Rock and Dime together. Judging by the traffic around the series of small workrooms, either daytime had arrived, the Seats had convened, or both.

"Hello," Rock offered.

Taking her lead, Dime joined in. "Good turn." She nodded. "Pleasant ways." One pyr actually waved back. With that, they took off, weaving past the surprised office workers in the direction Dime believed the complex entrance to be. They didn't slow down, and soon, Dime recognized the long, wide hallway, one of the forks stemming from the main entrance. That gateway was just ahead, just past the front vestibule. They were so close, they just needed to—

Neimano swung out into the vestibule, his black robes swirling with a storybook flair. "My Diamond," he intoned, as he strode down the corridor to stop right in front of them.

"Hi, is this the scheming leader you told me about?" Rock extended her hand. "Tootsy Wingclipper? *Ooh*, you're right. He's creepy."

"*Rock!*" Dime hissed. Well, now Neimano knew that she knew.

Rock dropped her hand with a shrug. "Sorry, he's nothing to me. I'm impressed by pyrsi who help others, not pyrsi who have all the power in the world and abuse it."

Dime's heart skipped as Neimano leaned in, almost touching Rock's face. "You will be laughing less when the brutes return under the control of the Seats." He spoke in a narrow voice, like he was talking to a ba'pyr.

He pivoted to face Dime. "Return that pendant. It's mine."

Dime felt the crystal turn cool against her chest, still hidden from view by her shirt. She wasn't giving him anything. "Let's go," she said to Rock. Neimano side-stepped, blocking them.

"Diamond, I'm sorry you were held in arrest. There was a grave misunderstanding. Let me put the brute back, and the full hospitality of the Seats will be given to you. I'll make it right. We have so much to discuss."

Should she play along? Take the chance to talk to him? Maybe she could learn more that would help. She'd have to bargain for and witness Rock's full release, of course. But her family—would it be worth more time away? Their worry?

Rock stayed silent. *Good.* She was glad Rock trusted her.

In that moment, something Ella had asked her to remember popped into her mind. Something about power of the powerful being that which pyrsi grant them.

There was room in the wide hall to walk around him; he couldn't detain them both. But then, would Rock and Dime harm him to get away? Even by pushing him, or wresting free of his grip?

The Violence. Not the Violence. Dime didn't know, but she wasn't going to let them put Rock back in that cage on a chance of what might happen. "Go around him."

Just as they edged around the winged, robed fairy, two of his High Guards appeared in the corridor behind him, alert as though they'd been trying to find him.

Neimano whipped around. "Assist me!" he yelled. "They are under arrest!"

He reached for Dime's arm and gripped his fingers around her wrist. Dime started to pull away, but then saw Rock tensing, ready to confront him. *No. No. No.*

Anger filled her, and frustration. She remembered the feeling.

And stopped.

"Rock, don't touch him," she urged. She closed her eyes, even as the guards rushed down the corridor toward them. She calmed herself, and thought about her friend, Rock, who had let her use the only mock key at the expense of her own freedom. Who'd then saved her life, almost at the expense of her own. With a friend like this, she was the luckiest pyr in the world.

Settling into that rush, she felt the valence inside her now. Free. It was in her; a part of her.

How could she end this assault, without harm?

It could be windy here.

A howling filled the air as wind from outside burst through the main gateway and turned into the long corridor. She slipped from Neimano's grip as each pyr leaned into the wind, trying to stay upright.

Dime split the wind into two, branching some of it outward, so it was easy for Rock and her to move again, toward the gateway. The second stream continued into the complex, making it easy for Neimano and his guard to walk away, but difficult for them to follow. Undeterred, Neimano continued to push against the wind, while his guards struggled, grasping at anything they could hold: grooves in the carvings or the bases of the glowstone lamps. Dime turned, and took Rock's hand; they ran, the wind at their backs.

Then the wind stopped, and Dime turned to see Neimano raising his hands. She whisked two statues from the sides of the hall and flung them into the center, just as a flash of light appeared from Neimano's direction. The teetering figures absorbed the brunt of whatever force Neimano had shot at them. They fell over and shattered, and Dime wrenched her gaze away from the destroyed art.

Determined, she dropped her backpack onto the floor. Sitting onto it, she pulled Rock awkwardly into her lap, and imagined the backpack wanted outside. Launching backward with Rock yelping in Dime's grip, they sped into the vestibule and spun out into the daylight, bumping past a host of chatting guards, and speeding right toward the forest trees. *We need to stop!*

The backpack thumped down onto a bed of low, flowered plants, looking worse for the wear but otherwise just a backpack. Both fe'pyrsi hopped to their feet and Dime slung the backpack on, just as Neimano appeared with his High Guards in the archway. The guards outside groveled and ducked, staring at their leader and awaiting his commands.

Pyrsi flying in, arriving for work, landed on the path. They stopped in an awkward cluster and gaped at the wingless visitors, goggling at the sight of their Third Seat towering at the common entrance, his hands raised in anger.

"He can't do anything here," Dime said, rushing the words out. "Even if he calls for our arrest, he can't risk them seeing me resist. He knows I'll resist. He can't risk them seeing me use valence. It's too complicated. Let's go."

Brushing themselves off, Dime and Rock walked into the dense trees. As soon as they were blocked from immediate sight, they ran, weaving an unpredictable path. "This way," Dime called. "Away from the city. We're at the edge." Her voice was growing thin. "It gets denser the further out you go."

Rock stopped, leaning against a tree, and Dime stopped with her. "I'm sorry, I've been in that box," Rock apologized, doubling over with heavy breaths. "No exercise!" She was rotating her shoulder, too. It must still hurt. Dime knew that any moment now, the High Guards would be crawling the skies, scanning for them.

"The staircase up is that way, along the cliff." Dime gestured. "He'll expect us to head toward it. We'll go this way instead and wait a while." She pointed at an angle to the cliff, a trajectory that would still keep them out of the city itself.

Rock nodded. "So, this is awkward, but I have to pee like a mountain deluge right now, and—"

"Harm, just go." Speaking of which. Dime almost jumped behind a tree, tossing her poor backpack to the side. Soon afterward, she joined Rock, emerging from behind another tree.

"That was close," Rock said, snapping her pants back together, with her torn shirt flapping behind her, almost like tiny wings.

"Don't tell my kids; I'm always lecturing them on it." Dime glanced up into the trees. "Let's try to find somewhere to hide and rest. It'll be hard to search the whole forest if he doesn't want pyrsi knowing we're here."

"It's too late for that, D." Rock grinned, but her usual lightheartedness didn't convey.

Rock followed the direction Dime had pointed, as Dime scanned the treetops for signs of dwellings and checked her compass wrist-piece, its needle bouncing in the direction of the cliff. As they got deeper into the woods, the path became more difficult, with thick growth and fallen branches obstructing their way forward. They worked with their hands, grunting to push heavy branches to form a path, or work through a blocked area. The fairies had found her last time because she was using valence to drive the car; she couldn't make that mistake this time. She cleared her mind and settled into only the sweat against her back and the textures of the brush against her sore fingertips.

"Your pal . . ." Rock said as they climbed over a fallen trunk, "do you think he'd actually harm us?"

There was nothing in Neimano's eyes that suggested repentance for what he'd done to her. Nothing that reached for understanding. "I think he might. I'd prefer not to give him the chance."

"Yeah. You know, I think he was lying about talking to you. I think he wants you gone."

Dime tried to consider what Rock meant. "What do you mean?"

"Not exactly sure, but I had a hunch about him. The way he looked at you. He's no longer interested in an alliance. Just . . . don't go with him."

Hmm.

Rock huffed as they continued to duck through the brush, seeking the paths with the most cover overhead. "Here." Rock pointed to one side.

Dime looked over at a fallen tree. Likely struck by lightning, its leaves remained thick and green, providing a broad canopy.

"Like our own tent," Rock wheezed, practically rolling inside as she gasped for breath.

Dime wasn't in much better shape. Every limb ached and pulsed as she stretched out onto the shaded ground, dragging her backpack beside her. "He can't search everywhere, right?"

Rock just groaned, sliding her own bag off to the side. They sat for much of a take, just catching their breath. Dime knew Rock was listening for sounds of pursuit, just as she was. Thankfully, the forest sounded only like a forest. Dime found herself getting lost in all the cracks and chirps and rattles. She closed her eyes.

"He won't find us now," Rock said. "As long as he keeps to his group."

She knew what Rock meant; that was her fear also. If Neimano decided to make a show of it, he could tell every pyr that the Ja-lal were loose on their lands. With that sort of panic, he could start the Great War right now. If he decided to stay low for now, he could order the dozen or so who had seen into silence. Then he'd only need them to obey.

Except, he couldn't be sure they would. Not *all* of them. A pyr who'd secretly disobeyed his own High Seat would be unlikely to hold such trust in others. "Who knew it was such a tinder box?" Dime voiced the thought aloud.

"Dawn's Circle?" Rock offered. Dime glanced over to see that her expression, dappled with specks of light filtering through the leaves, was serious. "I'm not taking credit for it; they recruited me, remember? I'm just saying I think we had some sense of the danger. That's why it was worth working two jobs, giving up our social lives, defying the Light."

They weren't directly defying the Light. If Sala didn't— No, she was thinking like the Circles again. It was defiance, what Rock did. What Ador did. What—

"Oh!" Rock shot up into a seat, almost bumping her head on a branch.

Dime sat up too, concerned. "Do you hear them?" she whispered.

"No! No! It's just, I finally remembered . . . what that reminded me of. Your statues. You flinging them like that."

"I have no idea what you're saying." Dime remembered this from before: Rock always assuming she could read her mind. Well, sometimes she could.

"Olok, the medic."

"Is this a novel?" Dime wasn't sure where Rock was going with this.

"No! She's a medic. Big deal a few cycles ago. A window cracked in one of the updated units. One of those big window frames; wasn't fitted right. The wood beams fell into the room, but by the time anyone arrived, they'd been moved away—tossed, it looked like— allowing the medics to get to a ch'pyr who was there for testing, and another medic, who must have been there tending to the ch'pyr.

"The IC heard about it and immediately opened a case, because if there were enough pyrsi there to move the beams, then there were witnesses who'd fled the scene. Or worse. Why would there be extra pyrsi in a room? Did their presence cause the accident somehow?

"And why was this well-respected medic there—Olok, who ended up in the enclave herself with huge cuts and bruises, or so they said at first. She couldn't explain what happened; just said she woke up that way and she must have been examining the ch'pyr when the wall caved in. But the ch'pyr was there for routine testing, so why would an expert like Olok be there?

"By the time they put together the interview list, case was closed. Olok remembered what happened, or more likely pulled some strings with her connections, and the agents were told to let it drop." Rock had picked up a little twig and was testing how far it could bend in her fingers.

"I wasn't involved in any of it; I was out on assignment. But it came up over a ferm when some of us were sharing stories. It made no sense, so agents talked about it for a while. We like things that make sense, as you know." She let go of the twig, which bounced out onto the ground.

It didn't take Dime long to realize where Rock was going with this. "And I take it Olok was my age."

"I don't know for sure, but she was a Bakh at the time. It fits. Except, now that you're saying we have valence too— Ugh." Rock rubbed her temples.

Dime shook her head. "If she caused the beams to move and was injured, that fits with untrained Fo-ror valence, and not with the Ja-lal ability to heal. Learning a ch'pyr was in danger could cause that sort of outburst. Except . . . I went through all the records from my birth cycle, and I would have at least paused on hers if it didn't have a natal exam. They don't add those in later, only right when you're born."

"Either you made a *mistake*," Rock looked at her pointedly, "or the extremely talented Olok, who actually worked in the enclave and got her own IC case closed, was able to forge this 'birth exam' and stick it in her file, just in case anyone got suspicious. And if that's true, that means she already knows."

"Wow." It wasn't the first time over the last several bells where Dime had felt her responses inadequate. She thought about Olok figuring it out, not knowing why or how, and just wanting to hide any evidence.

Dime hoped Neimano hadn't learned of the incident and tried to use or threaten Olok somehow. But if Rock hadn't considered it, Dime wasn't going to plant that seed. Olok was a victim either way, and according to Rock, she was still practicing in the enclave. The medic had been victimized enough; Dime wasn't going to make her a suspect as well. Letting it drop, she lay back against the ground.

When they'd rested and enjoyed a simple meal—though her loaf of bread was awkwardly shaped after one of them had apparently sat on it on the ride out of the complex—they decided to get some sleep also. Neimano could probably only search for so long, and the longer they waited to emerge, the more he'd have to expand the area he searched.

Dime slept well under the tent of branches, her body craving the renewed energy after the repeated use of valence. Rock appeared to have been awake a while when Dime finally dragged up and brushed herself off. Soon after, they'd packed up and were moving through the forest, back in the direction of the cliff. Dime and the generously-named cliff stairs were almost old friends by now. She was relieved to see no signs of anyone waiting there. No one in the sky. Their patience seemed to have paid off.

Rock had a basic set of climbing devices in her bag also, and so they were able, without too much challenge, to start the long trek from ledge to ledge, back up to the top. While climbing downward was more complicated, climbing upward was more strenuous and took at least three times as long. There was little conversation, between the physical exertion and the constant worry that a fairy might fly in out of nowhere, which stayed in both their thoughts.

They did rest once—they needed the break, but also Dime didn't know when or if she'd be back this way, and the upper ledges provided a simply stunning view. Together, they sat back away from the edge, concealed from view by taller shrubs. Dime hoped no one could see them here, and if they were out searching, she and Rock would have warning of their approach.

"So the secret is probably out now, right?" Rock had taken out her blade and was carving a knotted branch she'd found a few ledges below. "I mean, the fairies were seen in Lodon." She glanced at Dime. "The Fo-ror were seen in Lodon, and you and I were seen in Pito. So if anyone believes that breach would begin the war, then the war has begun. But—"

"But we don't want a war—" Dime filled in at Rock's prompt.

"Right. So you and I can pretend we're not involved in all of this, or we can try to," she made a gesture of her hands meeting, "guide pyrsi back together."

"How are you and I qualified to do that?" It wasn't a literal question, but Rock would understand that.

"We're all qualified to work it," Rock muttered. "It's just who's motivated and able to help."

"They're probably going to clean out my home when we don't pay the next bill." Dime would miss that wide ledge and those pretty windows. And all that beautiful wood and stone, she thought with a pang of homesickness.

"You wanted a change."

"I know, but not to become some exile, disliked by pyrsi who've never even met me. Not to fade from memory and still not be able to do anything."

"You're doing plenty." Rock's voice grew terser. "What about me? What do I have? Some crappy room rental. No homemates. No friends." She ran her hand along her forehead. "I don't even have my own tattoos. Who am I living for?"

Dime couldn't let it rest at that. Rock was part of what she now understood to be a critical movement. There were so many paths in life, she'd come to understand, and as long as society encouraged a—

"D. Are you growing hair? Sol, I thought it was just a weird reflection in the caves. No, you have actual hair. Are you going to keep growing it?"

From anyone other than Rock, that would be a pretty rude question. But Dime had increasingly understood these last turns that it was the unique closeness of friends, the ability to exist in one's most genuine form, that was the most valuable thing anyone could have. Dime grinned.

"I'm thinking about it. Here, wanna touch it?"

Grimacing, Rock set down the stick she'd been whittling and edged her hand over, acting like she was touching an old dish sponge as she ran one finger, gingerly, in an arc above Dime's ear. "Eww! It's weird and prickly!"

"Prickly, yes. Weird, not really. It's only weird because you've been told it's weird."

Rock sat back on the ledge, picking her blade up again. "What is *happening* to you?"

Looking out over the endless sky and with the forest below, Dime was tired of feeling like she was restarting this story again and again. All these events had happened. Some many turns ago, now. She'd seen new things and heard new things. At first, as they unfolded around her, and then because she'd sought them out. Her vantage had expanded. Her thoughts had changed. She didn't need *permission* to change.

"I know that I've been through things lately, and in some ways it's like we've just met. Or met again, I don't know. And it would make me feel better," she said, choosing her words with care, "if you just liked me for who I am now, and didn't try to make me sound like a hypocrite or something. Or a piece of the past."

Dime became worried when Rock didn't respond. She hoped the fe'pyr was just thinking.

"You're not a hypocrite. You never have been. It's more, like, watching a flower open. You can't help but notice . . . Oh, I'm sorry. That is so creepy. Let's try again— Actually, let's not. I get it. I'll try to be more careful. And then, maybe, you could stop talking to me like you're in charge here."

The momentary closeness stopped like a toothcar braking. "What?"

"I just . . . no, I'm not apologizing for it. I know you're the fairy, and I'm just the brute. You're the big to-do. But we used to work together, and I'd . . . well, you're right about the situation. And how unsettled pyrsi are. And how close we could be to the Violence returning. I'd like to work together again."

"I'd like that too." What had Rock said that felt wrong? She'd thought a lot about this, after all. "It's not the Violence returning," she clarified. "It's already here, right, always lurking. Maybe not war, or maybe not assault, but theft, pettiness, harsh words. Bullying over issues of perspective. There is no 'there or not-there' to it.

"So what's the cliff we're facing, if not that? In my opinion, it's the Violence being openly *sanctioned* again. Justified. Sometimes . . . sometimes I feel like when pyrsi say they fear the Violence returning, they're really saying they fear their *justification* returning. To openly declare aggressions rather than work to quell them. To employ the Violence, like it's a tool." She pointed down at her climbing hook.

"Or worse, to have to." Rock hugged her knees. "This view—"

Taking Rock's cue, Dime tried to relax and just take in the blues of the sky, painted over the vast treetops below: Sol's light shining down on the top of a whole society, its tree-based structures concealing as much as the tall towers of Lodon did of the lives lived within them.

It was nice to be here with Rock. She was still sorting through all the feelings she'd had around her, compounded by a difficult and emotional night and now day, but there was something in it she didn't want to lose again. And if Rock was willing to build a friendship, then maybe she wouldn't have to. That felt abrupt in such a short time, but she couldn't pretend it wasn't there.

Something else to figure out, she supposed, along with the peace and prosperity of the world. Dime looked over at Rock, not used to seeing her so pensive. "What are you thinking?"

Rock hesitated. "A lot. But most of all, what it would be like to see everything I've worked for get smashed to pieces. I'm not letting that happen."

In the shadows of the secluded ledge, or anywhere, Rock was beautiful. Her wistful eyes, and the seriousness of her passions. Her wit and humor. The way she wore that dirty, torn, blue shirt like a piece of fashion.

Dime said none of this as they packed up again and spent another bell making their way up the cliff.

Reaching the top, they pulled over the edge and crawled to a safe distance, Dime not sure she could have climbed much higher. Slowly, they stood and stretched. Every piece of her ached. "We're not young anymore." She glanced around, nervously. No one was in the sky. "We can't rest here, though. For obvious reasons," she added. Rock already knew that. She was more telling herself.

Sol's Reach stretched before them, in red and orange and shades of land. She felt as drawn to it as she'd been the green and violet Heartland just over the edge. A deep sense of protection gripped her, solidifying in her blood. Maybe Rock was right. In fact, Rock was eyeing her with an odd gaze.

"Ok. I won't give up valence yet," Dime said. "And I'll keep the pendant for now." What she did not add, but Rock surely surmised, was the amount Neimano's claim to it had factored into that decision. What she did add was how much Rock's own counsel had as well. "Thanks for talking. It's been a lot to deal with. As much as I continue to learn, there's so much I don't understand. So, thanks."

Instead of her usual quip, Rock looked serious—so much more mature than Dime remembered her. "I don't think one pyr can understand it all. That's why it's important to keep talking."

Talking. She'd been so caught up in getting into and out of the caves, she'd been distracted from her other goal, but now she wondered if Volana had reached the den to meet with Ador. Was she there now? Hope burgeoned again, settling her fears for the moment. She couldn't believe she hadn't told Rock. "Hey—I invited some Fo-ror I met to the den where we're staying. Just to talk about ideas. Come with me? You're welcome to stay with us a while."

Rock's chin lifted, then sunk. "No, I've had plenty Fo-ror for a bit. I need to get to the city for a while." Dime wasn't sure what to say, nor what to think about the way she didn't want Rock to leave.

Rock was leaving anyway. A thought occurred to her.

"I'd prefer you don't bother Olok. If she already knows, then maybe she's safe." Even if Olok should be told, Rock shouldn't be the one to tell her. Rock wasn't one of the victims, and she wasn't known for her sensitivity.

Her eyes flickered. "I will take that under advisement." Dime started to think what that meant, but Rock waved a hand. "Anyway. I've got to get back to the city." She squinted off at the horizon. "I need to be seen by Atti for a while. Put on a show like I'm bored and angry, and brief him on my last assignment. I do that every once in a while. He gloats. Suspicion is off me for a while and he doesn't notice how long I take to get things done."

Dime felt like she should have something to say, to part on a better note.

Instead, Rock touched her own lips and drew her fingers away, but didn't meet Dime's eyes. "See you soon, D. Promise."

Dime watched Rock walk away, further and further from her. She was waiting to wave, perhaps, but Rock never turned back. The shadows blurred under a thin cloud, and Dime remembered she had to get out of the open, certainly away from the edge of the cliff.

From where she stood, she could hike back to the den in only a bell or two. She missed her family, an increasingly present feeling these last cycles. It made sense; now that she knew the danger, she wanted to know they were safe. Dime appreciated them more than she ever had. Her friends as well.

Stretching, she watched a pack of wolgs bound across a series of plateaus. And, she'd sworn again and again, she was not traveling across any measure of the plains again without a *car*.

So, she decided, she was going to fly.

Interlude

Wonami's shovel hit something hard. Kneeling onto the fabric of her robes, she used a discarded shell to scoop away the sand. As long, light-colored arches emerged, she whistled in surprise: these were the bones of a newt.

That explained, she supposed, why the hill was bare of trees, and why boulders had been arranged around the clearing. She almost called for her spouse, who had flown off to find suitable timber, but stopped. What would he do? The animal bones were too close to the surface to allow a stable foundation for their new home, so they would have to be removed. Yet, they were still bones, so she'd treat them with respect.

They'd moved to Newt Lake to get away from the stresses of the city, while being able to enjoy the sense of community that had grown here. For a while, they'd tried a more remote place outforest, but living away from a village could be lonely, and sometimes the deliveries were unreliable. Wonami wasn't much of a gardener, and they'd gone without fresh greens one too many times when they heard about the growing settlements here.

Newt Lake was far enough away from Pito that the word had been slow to get out. They'd been thrilled to find there were still plots available—none so close to the lake, but within a quick flight. She'd been even more thrilled to find this clear patch of land, avoided by the others because of its lack of trees. Yet, seeing the flower-covered hill, lined with uniquely shaped boulders, Wonami felt she'd discovered a treasure. Ground-level homes were sometimes used in remote areas, and over time, trees would grow. A few had already peeked through.

She walked back to the lean-to they'd set up and rummaged through her things. Pulling out a large tarp and a bundle of rope, she tied the tarp around two fledgling trees, folding it over to create a pocket, of sorts.

The first bone extracted brought her a flap of awe. A rib bone, it was easily twice the length of her own. She held it against her chest, trying to imagine what she would be like with this size and strength. How grateful she was that the Seats had worked so hard to protect pyrsi from the unruly, yet majestic, beasts.

But, she supposed, it wasn't their fault for being what they were. Squips couldn't help being squips, and weed blooms couldn't help invading her attempts at a garden. Maybe she'd go see the newts herself, someday. Pyrsi said they lived in packs, out by the shores of blessed Sha.

Pulling each bone from the sand, one by one, she gingerly carried them to the tarp. Once she cleared what she needed to, she'd ask her spouse to help fly the bundle to Sha verself. They'd whisper a few words, and then lower them into the waves.

Wonami sat down, enjoying the breezes wandering up the hill, from the lake. Her mind danced with visions of a cozy house and a beautiful life, continued together. This was the nicest place she had ever been, and she was grateful to Sha that she'd claimed this spot first.

Act 3

GEMS

Her father's songs had lifted her up in other times of need, though never in such a literal context. And it was a specific song that came to mind now.

He'd written one, long ago, about a flying squip. Most of Da-da's lyrical fantasy sagas focused on exploring mythical lands and discovering fantastical creatures—but this one in particular was one of her favorites, because it was only about the squip's desire and will to fly.

> Squid the squip held his secret tight
> All the turns of his own passing life.
> Squid the squip just lived in his tree
> And all those turns he wanted to be
> More. Like a bird.
> Like the change in the wind.

She stopped caring for a moment that she wasn't supposed to be just standing in the open where any flying fairy, including Seat Neimano's guards, could easily locate her. Instead, she let go, and stood tall in the bright light of Sol, surrounded by the dusty winds of the sur plains. And she sang. She sang the intro, and the middle, and the part where Squid's naysaying friends make their last attempt to dissuade him.

All of Squid's friends lined up, like a wall
And warned that trying to fly, he could fall.
And Squid just turned his back to them all
And he jumped. And he knew. And he flew!

Like Squid, Dime didn't have wings to help her fly. But she now knew she could do it anyway, and she just had to figure out what would support her. She wasn't going to fly teetering on her backpack, even without any bread left to crush. Rock had said the fairies often used blankets or tarps to transport pyrsi or objects, but that required more cooperation with gravity than she was willing to risk.

She retraced her steps, carefully, toward the edge of the cliff, pulling up loose brush and sorting through the sticks that she found. Unwinding the rest of her climbing rope, for she wasn't worried about needing it for a while, she lashed the best sticks together into a rigid floormat like the ones she'd seen on the outer walkway of Yaliea's tree home.

Testing it, she was glad the structure didn't have much bend, but she did wish it had something she could sit against. She tied the loose ends of rope into a handle, not willing to strap herself directly to the contraption.

Staring at the mat, she remembered what had worked in the caves. It was different here, though she could still feel the caves underneath her. She focused on her own pendant. Instead of thinking about the branches, she tried to feel more comfortable with herself. More secure. She didn't worry about not having the other diamonds surrounding her. Her heart was enough. Her belief in herself. The mat rattled on the ground.

At that moment, she realized this was going to take practice. And work. And she settled in, not worrying about anyone out looking for her, and only worrying about where she was going. What she was trying to do.

After a while, the mat lifted, holding steady. Trying not to flinch, she concentrated and set it down again, repeating this a few more times. Next, she placed rocks onto it and then lifted those too. And then, finally, she sat down on the mat herself, her backpack behind her, and fingers gripped around the rope handle.

When compared to making magic, it was harder to overcome her own fear.

And when she lifted high enough that there was no more backing out, the mat still tilted and teetered, and Dime continued to focus. She continued to believe.

The thrill was such, at long last when she flew high above the cliff's edge, the forest to one side of her and the plains to another, that she decided not to make the short trip back to the den. Not yet. There was someone who might want to see this.

At this point, knowing that not believing would likely end her whole experience, she just kept believing. And she flew, wobbling around on the little mat and gripping the rope for her life, as amazing miniature landscapes unfolded beneath her. She flew nor and wes, until tall, pointed trees and grand ledges came into view. And in the far distance, she caught sight of something she'd never seen from Sol's Reach: *Sha*. A glimmer of blue twinkled beyond the land, past the old woods and its steep ledges.

And she thought that sometimes, maybe Suzanne would have flown this high, to peer out over Sha, and to know that both lands shared the same Sol, and the same Sha, and that even far away, she was still connected.

She tipped to the side and her backpack pulled at her, almost flopping her over the edge. Gasping, she heaved herself upright. And when she approached the tiny tower, at least tiny compared to the spires of Lodon, she almost flew right into it, swirling and knocking the top off of a pile of leaves as she skidded to a stop.

Ella was standing in the yard with a rake—which fell from her hand and landed with a *thunk* in the garden.

Dime had expected a different reaction. Claps of delight, tears of surprise, and especially a sarcastic reference or two. Ella's wide-eyed silence troubled her, as Dime followed her inside, and upstairs, where she gladly accepted a wet towel to wipe her face. The soft cloth wiped off rather grimy, but Ella just took it from her and turned to rinse it out.

"It's good to see you," Ella finally said.

"And you also. But . . . are you well?" Dime asked as she went to greet the plump-needled plant that Ella called Friend. Normally, one wouldn't ask about illness—even a close friend would tell you if xe wanted you to know—but generally offering a hand to someone who might need help was always proper.

"Me? Sure, just feeling down."

Those words concerned Dime, because there were all varieties of feeling down. There was having a quick illness down, or feeling bad about an uncomfortable exchange down, or just needing a break down. But it was also a code for pyrsi with serious emotional conditions who felt that asking for help would only burden others. Friends were not a burden. And she wasn't sure if Ella was down, or depressed.

Ella's expression answered that. Not for the first time, she wished Luja were here. Dime wasn't a medic. But she was a friend, and she knew that could help. Her own friends had provided so much of her strength these past turns.

Dime wasn't sure if Ella even had a medic she trusted. She knew Ella felt ostracized from the city, both because of the previous Light's cruel propaganda against her and because of Ja-lal society's prejudices against the Fo-ror. To Dime, the tall stone towers of Lodon represented accomplishment—the heart and strength of the Ja-lal. To Ella, they represented rigidity. Division. Walls. Yet, Ella had a few friendly contacts in the city, and she went there on occasion.

"Let me know if I can do anything for you," Dime offered.

"I do appreciate that. It's nice of you to stop by."

Dime remembered, with a pang, that she could no longer just stroll back into the city to coordinate with a medic. And maybe, having been seen near the fissure, Ella couldn't either. She hoped she hadn't done that to her.

Her own heart sunk as she noted Ella's dulled reactions. She wished she knew how to help. She thought back to some of her own dark turns, back when the weight of her situation within the Circles fell too heavy on her, and she'd sat for bells mostly staring at the wall. The best help she'd had then was the pyrsi who'd supported her. Who'd let her know she mattered to them.

It wasn't a cure, but maybe that's what Dime could offer. She shifted her tone.

"I wanted to come see you, before I went to the den. I haven't been back yet, since visiting the caves. As far as I know, Dayn and Luja are still there." She decided not to mention Tum, as Juni and Tum were clearly not here, and the uncertainty of whether Tum was still safe with the newts might be upsetting to Ella as well. "My friend, Ador, he implied you knew each other, is there, along with another of the Free Winds. And I invited a couple of the Fo-ror to come meet us."

This at least got Ella's interest. "Which Fo-ror?"

Dime didn't think Ella expected to know random Fo-ror by name, so she assumed the question regarded affiliation or rank. Given Dime's previous casual references to meeting Ferala, Ella might not put much past her. But there was a more important issue to address, and maybe this would help. "If you'd like—you could stay at the den a while. Just a visit. Maybe being around others would help. I know it's a help to me."

"I'm fine," Ella said. "Been through worse. And which Fo-ror did you invite? Don't say Ferala."

Dime smiled, not wanting to push her. The offer would stand. "No, not Ferala, though I do have one of his pens." Ella squinted. "I met a pyr associated with the Foundry; are you familiar with it?"

"I am," Ella answered, appearing to let the pen comment go, "but I think they've grown over recent cycles. Suzanne was generally sympathetic to them, but once we moved here, she didn't often go back to the forest. If she did, it was to fly outforest; she was never one for the city." Ella glanced away.

"The pyr I invited wasn't sure she was right for the discussions," Dime said. "She implied she was low class. I guess she cleans as her role. Others bullied her over it the first time we met." She bristled, remembering their taunts, which would have been considered the Violence anywhere she'd ever been. The Ja-lal had flaws, but they'd never disrespect someone for xyr profession. "I took to her immediately; she seemed especially smart and compassionate. Someone I'd want to work with."

"Interesting. I'm not saying don't do it, of course—frankly the idea has me hurrahing—but take care ignoring Fo-ror class too far. There are ingrained feelings about it, more than even a Lodonite would understand."

Dime caught the barb of Ella's remark. The limitations weren't as strict, but Lodon placed great weight on class as well, much more than the rest of Sol's Reach. She was suddenly embarrassed for the narrowness of her previous thoughts and was glad she hadn't voiced them. She believed strongly in civility, but it never justified inequity.

Ella put her hands against the side of her thighs. "Are we avoiding the squash in the bean patch here?"

What?

"You did get here on a flying raft?"

"Ah, yes, I did. And it was terrifying, so I'd like to borrow a chair for my next attempt."

"Of course you would. So, you went to the caves. It all worked."

"It did." Dime wasn't ready to talk through the details. Her recurring resentment of her pendant continued to poke at her, fueled by one underlying thought. As easily as valence had come to her, it could just as easily—and had at least twice—hurt others. "I managed it just fine."

"You sound like you didn't expect to."

There was more truth to that than Dime had allowed herself to form into thoughts. But, yes, part of her had hoped she wouldn't be able to make it work and she could go back to being a regular wingless pyr. It sure seemed less scary that way.

"The caves are stunning." Dime couldn't help her surge of awe at the memory of the sheer number and size of crystals lining room after room. "So much more than I expected."

"I can't even imagine." Ella's tone suggested it was a literal statement.

"There's something else I think I learned there," she added. Ella waited.

"I don't know if you've ever had surgery to your back." Ella didn't have to answer this, though she shook her head. "There may be a tissue lining a Ja-lal's inner back that is . . . the same as wing tissue."

Ella swung a chair over and sat down.

"So, yeah," Dime continued, "I think . . . we all have valence. We all have a heart, right? The Fo-ror have learned to let theirs grow outward—like the trees they live amongst—to affect the world around them. So, here's my theory. The Ja-lal have this tissue inside. They've learned to direct that energy inward, like—like the stone they live amongst. For stamina, strength, healing—maybe even for innovation. Except, just like I didn't use valence when I didn't know I could, Ja-lal don't know they can either."

"So they don't," Ella said, without inflection. "I . . . I have examples as well. I believe it's true. I'm . . . confused why I've never considered it."

Dime understood and at the same time was over that type of argument. "I just learned in mid-life that I not only have powers but am decent at using them. We're all so limited by what we believe or believe to be possible. By what we've been told or haven't. I'm tired of discovering new ideas and being frustrated at why I didn't discover them before. I'd rather just *discover* them."

"I'm still paging through what Ja-lal valence could mean." Ella's glassy stare indicated she was absorbed in thought.

"Oh, no worries. Just break into the fairy complex, go past the prison and into the caves, and you can knock it out pretty quickly."

They both started to laugh, and Dime was glad to see Ella's smile, even if fleeting. "Well, come on! That's the advice you gave me!"

"You took it, didn't you? Then flew here on a clothes dryer?"

"I did." Dime pressed her hands together a couple times, because this part was a little hard to say. "There's something else, that I think Luja tried to tell me, back before I left. Ve was asking me about wing tissue, and then said ve thought of something, or—I don't remember exactly what happened except I thought ve was going to talk about my biology in front of this relative stranger, and I—"

"Would ve have done that?" Ella never minded interrupting when she thought something was important.

"Aochs aren't known for discretion."

Ella sighed. "I know I'm overstepping my bounds here, but if you continue to treat ver like a ch'pyr, ve's going to start resenting you."

"Oh, ve's fine. Ve—"

"I spent a few bells with ver, and I can tell the youth is bursting at vis seams. Trust is so important at that age. I'm sure even Dime the Gamh remembers."

She tried not to, sometimes.

"Pyrsi vis age are unripe; I know that. My advice—as a friend—is to keep that understanding to yourself, and let ver feel your encouragement and trust instead. Otherwise you'll end up pushing ver to somewhere you won't like. I've seen it before." She paused. "And I'm trying to help."

"Thanks." Ella's words had hurt to hear. Dime wanted to be a good mother. She thought she did trust her children. And if there was truth in Ella's lecture, she'd want to sort it out in private, not here with her emotions on her face.

"I worry about this Ja-lal valence." Ella's face was drawn. "We put enough pressure on ourselves as it is. To be strong. To heal. Even to be tall—even if it causes us to teeter on huge shoes."

Dime cut Ella a warning look. Fine, Dime did tend to brag about never wearing heels, but part of it *was* that pressure. How many pyrsi had passed her over, assumed her level of competence, just because she wore comfortable clothes, or didn't wear makeup, or didn't wear heels.

"We put so much pressure on ourselves as Ja-lal," Ella continued. "Sol's pyrsi, strongest of Ada-ji. Maybe I'll try valence; maybe I won't. But I don't have the focus to heal myself right now, or even the inclination to try, not knowing what the outcome could be. One thing Suzanne made very clear about Fo-ror valence is that it varied. Throughout life or based on circumstances. Not everyone has the same knack for it, and even equal strengths can manifest in different ways.

"So what now, we have to deal with valence too?" Ella pressed her fingers against her cheek. "Don't be depressed; you have valence. Just fix it!"

Dime was sure there were more examples, but that first, and hardest hitting one, stopped Ella from offering any more. As Ella slumped forward onto her hand, Dime thought about Zael, who had expressed the same sentiments without even understanding there could be valence behind them. He'd said everyone told him he could do it; he could defeat his illness if he "thought positive" and "fought it." *What a well-intentioned cruelty, to be told you can cure a condition by someone who doesn't know if you can.*

They sat quietly, only the birds chirping outside. Yet, the mention of Suzanne had tickled something in Dime's thoughts. At first she couldn't remember, then realized it was an idea she'd had while in the Heartland.

A series of sketches lined the wall of Ella's primary living floor where they now sat. Some sketches lined the third floor, and she'd only briefly seen the fourth, which Ella kept private. The sketches were expertly created, of a diverse set of plants, many of which Dime was sure grew only in the Heartland. She'd been meaning to ask. "Did Suzanne draw these?"

Suzannelina, Dime recalled, was her full name. Ja-lal might shorten the longer Fo-ror names, finding the shorter names more comfortable to say or remember. But after hearing them spoken with such ease in the Heartland, the Fo-ror names felt natural to Dime. She'd never correct Ella, of course, but in her mind she imagined Suzannelina of the outforest. Except she couldn't imagine her. Which was the thought she'd had.

"I did," Ella answered. "Suzanne liked to write, not to draw. We always said we'd make a book together. We never did."

Ella drew them. Dime was surprised she hadn't considered it. But, why not? Then, even more so, there was a picture. There had to be.

Asking about it was intimate. Dime hoped not too far. It just felt like . . . she'd grown so close to Ella, yet Suzannelina was part of her. And Dime wanted to meet that part just a little, if she could. "I'll completely understand if you choose not to answer, so please forgive me. Do you have a drawing of her?"

It took a stride for Ella to answer, and Dime fretted that she'd overstepped.

"She would like for you to see it, I think," Ella said, motioning for Dime to follow her upstairs. They wound around past the sleeping area, and up into the divided library nooks of the top floor. Ella stepped behind a bookcase. A large cushion sat on a low pedestal, in front of a broad window. Behind, an ebonized bookshelf curved around, filled with books.

Sol streamed in, throwing streaks of light across the cushion and the smaller pillows arranged into a neat pile on top. Beside the window hung a portrait. Dime walked over to it in silence.

A round face gazed back at her, drawn so expertly it could have been a window to a real pyr. Light gray skin, no tattoos, and a mass of curly hair, mostly a natural white, but streaked with a few artful touches of pastel dyes—perhaps made from the juice of berries. Little flowers accented the tight curls, some dark violet and others a periwinkle blue. One large streak was rose pink. Suzannelina's gold-flecked eyes twinkled with wit and delight, and behind her, purple wings rippled, out of focus.

Instead, the focus was on her eyes, which glimmered over a wide nose and a slightly upturned mouth, with a touch of humor to it. Not a sarcastic humor, but the look of loving one's life. Of loving every detail and nuance of it, no matter what trials it threw.

"Thank you," Dime whispered, "for sharing her with me."

From Ella's mention of illness and expectation, it seemed Suzannelina had died young. Too young, anyway. She didn't know why. It wouldn't be right to ask. The fact that she'd lived, in the past, and here every day, in this image and in Ella's heart, was something Dime would carry with her.

It also reminded her that her own spouse was waiting for her at the den. She should get back to the others, who would be worried. And she wanted to know whether Tum had returned, also. But she waited until they were back in the living area with a cup of brew, and she'd told Ella more about her experiences in the caves.

She almost left then, but Ella seemed to be cheering with Dime's company. So she stayed longer. They walked in the garden, looking for seeds. Returning inside, they played a game.

Only then. "I need to get back. You're welcome to come with me."

Ella bowed her head. "I need to stay here."

Dime stood and went to rest her hand over Friend's sprawling, green needles. "Goodbye for now, Friend. I'll be back."

She turned to Ella. "Could I borrow one of your chairs?"

"You're going to make it fly?"

Dime grinned.

"Fine. I pick the chair; I soup it up." She rose with a bit of a spring to her step and pointed at the staircase. "And you need to give me your flying floor mat in exchange for my generosity. It would be perfect in my entry way. Perfect. It's like you measured it."

Dime appreciated the reference to Fo-ror barter. And she was flattered Ella knew, by the way she'd said it, that Dime would understand. "I'd be honored to give you my floormat. Hand-selected brush, from the very edge of the cliff." That was fitting, she supposed.

A take later, when Dime returned from using the bath, she heard a sawing sound in the yard. Amused, she saw Ella had taken a wide, rather aged chair, and was fitting scrap boards into . . . what was she making?

She watched with interest as Ella eventually constructed a lidded box onto the back of the chair, large enough for Dime's backpack and even a few miscellaneous items.

As Ella wiggled the last board into place and then set a nail against it, she looked up at Dime. "My wrists are bad. You push them in as I set them." *Push them in?*

Realizing what she intended, Dime felt a sharp flash of aversion, a voice saying *no* inside of her, worried at influencing the sharp little objects. She was so close to saying that she couldn't. And if it were anyone else here, Rock or Ador or Dayn, she would have. But Ella glanced up with expectant eyes.

It took less thought than it might have. One after another, the nails pushed in. A few not far enough, and Ella tapped those down, and a few definitely too far. Ella ignored them.

"There," she said, giving the chair a final pat.

Shaking off what she'd just done, Dime inspected the chair, raising and lowering the thin lid over the storage behind it. Ella had used whatever hinges she had, and none of them matched, yet for something so tossed together, it was welcoming.

The chair was broad enough that she wouldn't be pinched in it. She started to laugh as Ella began to weave a heavy belt under and back around. "You have no wings," Ella reminded with a lilt as she rested each side of the belt onto the chair's seat. Almost skipping back into the tower and returning with another wet towel, she wiped down the surface, cleaning off any loose sawdust.

"I'd stain it properly, but we'll have to wait for next time."

"Yes, I really should get back. I hope that all is well at the den, but I can't know that." *And Tum.*

Ella squinted. "Don't be naïve. That's all."

Rather blunt. But without any humor in Ella's tone, Dime only nodded.

After a few more words and a tight hug, Dime loaded her backpack into the storage bin, cinched herself into the chair, and lifted back up, wavering in what was no doubt a comical pattern. *Ack.*

Dime avoided getting too close to the trees as a bird squawked in protest. "Sorry," she whispered.

Ella stood at the edge of her tower, waving until Dime was out of sight.

Dime would have to work on landings. But at least no one saw this one, as she bumped down a bit over from the den entrance, catching herself on her hands as the chair tumbled forward. Muttering as she flipped herself upright, she skimmed, just above the ground, until she got to the den's front. No one would be outside the hidden entrance, so without the added pressure, she skidded to a pretty reasonable stop.

"Ma-ma?" a voice called.

Tum was sitting in the dirt, drawing shapes with a stick. Almost forgetting to unbuckle, Dime rushed over to sit next to her, sweeping the young fe'pyr into her arms.

With wide and glistening eyes, Tum looked up at her mother like she was the coolest pyr in the world. Dime captured the image, one she'd never forget. Having forgotten how heavy her child had become, she set her back down, wobbling a bit.

"Did you just fly on a chair?"

"I did," Dime said with a wink. "I told you I was born Fo-ror. Turns out, I can use valence too." After having to tell pyr after pyr each new revelation over the past turns, Tum's open acceptance, that of course her mother could use valence, was incredibly comforting.

"Now we both have chairs," Tum said, bouncing on her arms.

Taken aback, Dime considered this. "Yes, I suppose we do. But yours is nicer!" It was no offense to Ella's quick craftspyrship, but Dayn had built their child a masterpiece.

"It's the best," Tum agreed.

"So, how was it?" Dime wanted to see the others, but—her child had lived among the newts and no matter how much she trusted them, she was worried for Tum's experience, especially at this age. "Did you go to their beach, or did Juni stay in the old woods?"

"We went to their homes; I think they call them beds. They are so great there. Everyone liked me and the ones who didn't I just made them like me anyway. Juni was so fun, and we went to the water—did you know the Sha is real?—and we worked on her burrow, and I helped her make a sled, to pull food, and I showed her how to use it, and we learned to play games, and she showed me new berries and roots, and I got her to teach me some of their words, and—" Tum paused for breath. It didn't last long.

"You aren't going to believe this! Juni has a fancy green lizard, and I think she said it was from you. She keeps it right at the front of her burrow, and she pets it and coos. Is that true? Did you give Juni the lizard? I think that's what she said."

"I did." Dime grinned, but with a guilty memory about the circumstances. Inadvertently, the gift had provided young Juni elevated status among the troop, or at least indicated to the others that Dime saw her that way. Upon learning this, Dime had offered their leader, who Dime called Stern Eyes, their food for the return trip to try and make up for it. She still felt bad about the cultural misstep. Before then, she didn't even know animals had cultures to misstep.

"Ma-ma, do you know what the best part was?"

Dime thought it might be seeing new sights. She remembered the first time she'd seen Sha in the daylight, reaching out without end, with its glittering—

"*I ran for the first time.* In Juni's arms, of course, but we ran. Not like how I do it, but *fast*. When I told her how much I liked it, we did it all the time. Running to the forest, running to the water. Running to food. Juni's like me; she doesn't get tired. So we ran and ran and ran!"

Running. Questions formed in Dime's mind about Tum's stay, but Tum had already bounded ahead, on her hands. Sitting back, she held the door open as Dime struggled to wiggle Ella's large, heavy chair down the stairs. Dayn's arms reached out and helped her carry it.

"I'm back," Dime offered, touched at the clear relief in Dayn's expression to see her safe.

His gaze turned to the chair, trying to puzzle it out. Starting, he almost fell back against the table. Dime leaned in against his ear. "I totally did." He could only shake his head as Dime grinned. "I learned a lot. But mostly I missed you." They leaned in for a quick but strong kiss, holding it just one moment longer, before turning to face the small, bustling room.

Ador and Luja had been playing the squip game, and Hin sat reading against a wall. They all rose, seeing Dime, with Tum clinging to her side. They greeted each other with waves and smiles, though Ador stayed back as Luja rushed vis mother, enveloping her in a huge hug. Behind ver, Agni raced in circles, mewing. Dime bent to scratch behind her ears, and the kita flopped to the ground with a contented purr.

"I'm so glad to see you all," Dime said, her heart filling with joy, enough that she was glad to just forget everything else for the time. For a little while.

"Ma-ma," Tum swung over to a cushiony chair, and Dayn helped lift her into place. Agni jumped up with her, curling into a ball. "Can I see them again?"

There was no question who she meant. "I think so, Tum."

Tum bounced excitedly as Dayn's eyes showed his continued relief and wonderment at Tum's newt stories as well as how obviously happy she'd been with them.

"Here, I have something for us, when we find a new home." She pulled Rock's carved owl out of the bag. Hin set down his book, and edged over. "Go ahead," Dime offered, seeing his interest.

Hin ran a hand along the owl's back, finally caving and picking up the heavy object. "Is it—"

Dime realized, after the carved squips, he might think that it was from the Fo-ror. "It's by my friend from Lodon. I left to go help her."

"Oh." He smiled. "It's wonderful. She really knows how to work with the natural lines in the wood. And what is that?" A smaller object was lying sideways on the table, where it must have fallen when Dime retrieved the owl.

As dark in color as the owl was, this piece of wood was light, shaded with almost yellow hues, like daylight. It was a seated figurine, small and rough-hewn. Even without detail, the unpolished carving evoked a very real sense, much like an abstract painting implied detail it didn't contain. Dime recognized the figure as herself, staring out over the forest when they'd sat on the ledge.

"Oh, that's my good luck charm," she said, slipping it into a pocket. She sat the owl in the center of the table. "There."

An awkward silence followed, as leaving on her own and returning with a carved owl didn't speak to why she'd left. What was the plan, now that Dime had returned? Would they stay here, squatting in an IC den? Tum still had her classes in the city. Luja had been actively seeking apprentice work as a medic. Dayn had his career. All in the city.

Ador and Hin could return to Lodon at any time, except they were here, waiting for the arrival of the fairies, for an initial dialogue. She supposed that was the next step, for now, and she'd have to figure out the rest, soon. The look she exchanged with Dayn suggested he understood. That calmed her.

She scanned their faces, confirming her assessment. "I take it the Fo-ror have not arrived?" Volana had said she had a work shift to complete, and also that Uchitar needed to recover for the flight, and they'd leave within a turn. So, either they'd be here soon, or they'd decided not to come. Not thinking the latter likely, Dime was glad she could be here for their arrival.

"They have not," Ador answered. "I admit, I've been excited to meet them. Who did you invite?"

"Fo-ror society has a strictness to class structure that we don't,"

Dime began. Luja half-snorted. "No, it really does. Our feelings on class drive how we view one another, but don't strictly limit where a pyr may enter or end up. Remember, this is what's had the Sol's Pillars so bothered. Until they found this latest outlet, anyway."

Hin shifted at their mention. Well, she wasn't a fan either, but that didn't mean they should stop talking about them.

"I found a pyr that I just . . . trust. And another I do too, though he's having a bit of trouble. I just wanted to warn everyone so we could be understanding."

"Trouble?" Dayn asked.

"Tzetz addiction."

Luja's head dropped and Hin glanced away. Ador and Dayn pursed their lips, in a similarly sympathetic grimace.

"Isn't that bad?" Tum asked.

"It's difficult. And very rough on mind, body, and relationships. I wanted you to understand if he seems out of sorts."

"Does he have the hemsa?" Luja asked.

"The Fo-ror don't have tattoos. Or hemsa." Luja and Tum glanced at each other in surprise, and Hin leaned back in his chair. Dime turned back to Ador. "The other pyr is active in something she called the Foundry. You've heard of it?"

Ador grimaced. "Not exactly. The pyrsi we've had contact with will discuss Fo-ror culture all turn with us, yet nothing related to their government. It's a line they don't like to cross."

"I don't know much myself, but it sounds somewhat similar to the Free Winds."

"Excellent. Though—you started by talking about class?"

Dime nodded. "Volana, the Foundry member, was set to send someone else here. I believe she cleans, and that's considered low-class."

"Anyone who cleans for me might as well be the Light," Dayn murmured. Dime laughed. He wasn't making a joke about the profession, Dime knew. He was poking at how much the pair of them disliked basic cleaning. Luja, on the other hand, was meticulous, probably picked up from vis medic training. And so it was a running inside joke that when Luja kept everything tidy, they didn't go out of their way to point out the inequity.

Luja, tapping vis fingers against vis mouth, seemed deep in thought, quite oblivious to vis chuckling parents.

"I look forward to meeting them," Ador said, not seeming to get Dayn's joke. "And thank you for the warning on Fo-ror class. I had a sense of that also, but there's so little we know about them, and they're so guarded on these subjects."

In terms of insight, Dime was regretting not pushing Rock to return with her. Rock should have been here—she was part of Dawn's Circle, dedicated to understanding the Fo-ror. She suspected the Free Winds didn't even know about Dawn's Circle. But it wasn't her secret to reveal. And Ella, she could have added so much.

The others became quiet again. No one resumed their activity, as if maybe Dime had more to say. Did she? Everyone here but Hin was aware that she was biologically Fo-ror, and everyone but Hin knew she had just gone to teach herself the basics of valence. She didn't want to treat him like an outsider, but he'd previously expressed discomfort with the idea of the Fo-ror, so she wasn't ready to tell him yet.

Once he met the others, she hoped, he'd start to relax about the idea. She imagined this would be the case with many Ja-lal.

"Here, let me make us some food," Dayn said, rising to light the small stove. As the clang of bowls and the chopping and sifting of ingredients filled the room, the others broke into smaller conversations. Relieved a bit, Dime plopped down at the table.

It was nice, for a while, not to talk about the changing world and how she fit into it. Instead, Hin told her how he'd found and joined up with the Free Winds. He wouldn't outright say it, but she had the impression the discussion on class had affected him significantly. From the way he spoke, familiar to her, he'd probably grown up in a low-class family too. His accent didn't ring of the city, though, like Dime's did.

She asked where he was from, and he described a small village in the hills. He missed his siblings, he said. His tenor rose when he talked about the Circles, and the peace he had found joining the Free Winds. "Pyrsi have a right to be free," he said, eyes blinking.

"I agree," Dime said. "Maybe we can help with that."

"I hope so," he agreed.

They exchanged a smile, and Dime felt sympathy for the young pyr, who must have felt a little out of place around the others here, as close-knit as they were.

Later, after Luja had cleaned up what was left of a superb roasted stuffed cabbage, and Dime had sipped a glass of citrus tea over a bell or two of conversation, finally did she admit she couldn't go another stride without some rest.

Just as she snuggled into the bed, Luja and Tum both peeked through the doorway. "Ok, ok, just shut the door," she said. She sat up as they both joined her.

"Tum says you flew here on that chair." Luja leaned in.

"I sure didn't carry it." *I mean, if you can't brag to your kids—*

"Can we see some?"

Dime sighed. After a slight lecture during which she explained it was important not to potentially draw pursuers to them with the use of valence, she did take a yarn ball they'd made for Agni and bounced it around the room, making the yarn wave in cute patterns, with only a few awkward flubs. Nervous, she glanced around for the kita, but clearly Agni hadn't followed the others into the room.

The thought crossed her mind that she should not say the next thing she said. But Ella's lecture about treating Luja like a ch'pyr felt fresh, seeing Luja's expectant face. And, if she were really going to think of ver as a grown ji'pyr, she should probably realize Luja already suspected. Better for ver to have facts. And caution.

"Luja, I have to apologize for interrupting you, when I was here before. The wing tissue. On the inside. You were correct about it. At least, I think that's what you were saying. I agree."

Luja mouthed *wow* and Tum bounced on the bed, annoyed to be left out. Dime raised her hands toward both of them, lowering her voice. "I'm saying I think Ja-lal can use valence too. My theory, though don't let this limit your research, is that Ja-lal use their valence internally."

"Like healing, right?" Luja scrunched vis face.

"Yes," Dime answered. "I've . . . I've seen that, actually. But maybe strength or stamina too. I wonder how much of Ja-lal medicine focuses subconsciously on inherent power that we hold. That you hold," she corrected. "For me, this explains a lot."

"I think valence is love!" Tum declared. Dime made a shushing gesture, thinking of the small dwelling. Tum sat back, pouting.

"It's not that simple," Luja lectured. "It's complicated."

"Let's not argue," Dime said, lots of ideas now occurring to her.

"If pyrsi have valence that heals them," Luja mused, "why do pyrsi get hurt? Why do they die?"

Dime thought of Zael, perhaps dying in Lodon—all the while, being urged by pyrsi he loved to take care of it himself. She thought of Fo-ror valence, as well, with such immense potential for power, yet a society deferring that power to tradition. "I think," she said, "we all have powers beyond what we know. And, perhaps, understanding that those powers do and should have limits is just as important as believing in them in the first place."

"The Free Winds say no pyr should have too much power," Luja said. "Hin's always spouting that stuff." Luja didn't look thrilled by this. Used to Ador's devoted treatment, it might be strange for ver and Tum to split his attention with someone new. Especially if that someone was often lecturing ver.

"I do think I agree," Dime yawned. "And now you've got a few more things to think about. I'm sorry, but can Ma-ma get some rest?" They each gave her a peck on the cheek, and exited silently. As the door closed, Dime could hear Agni squeaking in protest, followed by the thump of Tum tossing her the little yarn ball.

"Hey," Dayn whispered through the door. "Hey, sleepy. Your, uh, fairies are here."

"Hmm?" The door was already closed, but Dime was fairly sure she'd heard what she'd heard. Taking the side door to the bath, she threw on another set of clothes—one of her old familiar velour suits she'd taken from Lodon—and almost reached for her razor. Grinning, she set it down.

Dayn and the kids had all said they didn't care if she grew hair or not. Tum wouldn't care if she grew fur like a kita, and Dayn, understated as always, had said it would be "interesting to see." Luja had even agreed with Hin that it was cool and had called her "totally counterculture," which Dime still didn't know how to take.

Except, leaning into the mirror, she saw a hint or two of hair on her eyebrows.

Too far! She carefully shaved those off.

It was surreal seeing Volana greeting each pyr in the living space, one that now looked quite cramped. Meanwhile, Uchitar hovered by the wall, his eyes uneasy and his wings almost dragging against the low ceiling. Dime went straight to him.

"Uchitar, I'm so happy to see you again. Welcome to Sol's Reach." She extended a hand, waiting for consent to rest it on his arm. Instead, he grasped and held it, thinking that's what she meant to offer. He seemed to calm at the touch, so Dime gave his hand a squeeze.

"Your houses are fancy," he said.

Dime tried not to laugh. From the little she'd seen of the tree homes in Pito, they were each decorated like little nature museums. Here, the wallpapered IC den felt not much nicer than one of the Seats' diamond cages. But, she realized, there was probably something she didn't see here. Something that appealed to Uchitar differently.

She glanced around, taking in the elaborate stove and metal shelving racks. The burning lamps. She saw it with new eyes. "Thanks," she told Uchitar. "It isn't ours, it belongs to our Circles, like your Seats."

Uchitar removed his hand by instinct. "What will they do?"

"It's all sort of upside-down right now, anyway. I'm trying to figure it out."

He turned to her with a warm smile, his wings folding behind him. "I get that. We can't stay long, though. At nightfall, Volana has her longest break between shifts. It took us a while to find you."

Dime, annoyed, realized that between her long sleep and the lack of windows, she didn't even know it was night, or had been for a while.

Meanwhile, Volana was already engaging in conversations around the room. Dime was glad to see the casual way Volana leaned down to speak privately to Ador, and was curious whether that was difficult for her to do. If class was a concern in the Heartland, Ador exuded class. Volana wouldn't know that his status was diminished with the Circles. Unless, Dime supposed, he told her.

Fully introduced and with a pot of fresh brew on the table, they pulled a set of chairs around. Their chairs here were all backed, but the two Fo-ror opened their wings flat behind them. The pyrsi on either side scooted their chairs slightly away to accommodate. They shifted to crowd around, even with Tum still sitting in a chair by the wall, and Luja and Uchitar moving slightly away, to allow space.

Dime didn't know if it was polite for Luja and Tum to listen in—or at least Tum—but what, would she send her into a bedroom only for her to listen anyway?

Maybe a Ja-lal could enhance their hearing with valence, she thought. She glanced suspiciously at Tum. Tum, seeing her pointed stare, just grinned.

"So how are you connected to your Seats?" Hin was asking, his gaze flitting a bit between the two fairies. She hoped while she'd been gone Hin had adjusted more to the idea of meeting the Fo-ror. Or at least, of being open to it.

Volana answered, her voice shaking just a little. "The Seats don't know we are here. The Seats would not authorize this." She paused, the silence potent. "Dime said you were with a group, and you'd be interested to talk."

"And we are," Ador confirmed. "I'm so honored that you would travel here, at great risk, just to talk to humble members of Ja-lal society such as we. And if I could be so bold, I would ask you first, do you feel the tension in your land that we do in ours? The boundaries of peace, about to snap?" Ador's voice and words, as always, were smooth and elegant.

"I'm just a cleaner," Volana said, though her chin rose.

"Burgess Volana, you are a representative of the Foundry, and I, as a representative of the Free Winds, am requesting your help, if you would provide it." Ador's expression held its intensity. Uchitar sat up straighter.

"The Free Winds? This is your name?"

Ador nodded.

"In our culture, a free wind is a sign of danger. Of staying put until things settle." Seeing Ador's surprise, she quickly added, "I'm sorry, I meant it not as judgment."

"Let's consider it a sign. A sign of how much we have to learn about each other. For in Sol's Reach, a Free Wind speaks to a drift that might upset the way something stands. The danger is to tradition, not to pyrsi."

Volana raised a finger to her lips. "Maybe . . . the Fo-ror could stand to try flying in this wind."

"Or maybe, we could change our name."

In a clear moment of connection, Volana and Ador beamed across the table at one another, as Dime and the others watched in amazement.

"To your question," Volana quickly regained her composure, "I do feel this worry, as you describe. I hear talk of the brutes, now, even amongst the burgesses of the canals. They did not speak this way before. And so, oddly, it did not surprise me to see Dime, wingless and hairless, with her face marked. My friends, there, they often . . . have a sense of things first."

Dime thought, in light of those comments, that perhaps she should be open with Volana about her story. But not here, in the middle of the meeting.

"In the Foundry, we question—"

There was visible effort in whatever Volana was about to say in front of complete strangers. Dime admired the pyr's bravery. She and Dayn met eyes, as Volana started again.

"In the Foundry, we question the level of control and authority that the Seats hold over pyrsi. What they call *tradition*, that we take as unchangeable. It is said that Sha provides these leaders with our wishes and needs, enabling them to take care of us. And we are taken care of, by any measure." Volana's volume grew, as did the conviction in her voice. "Taking care of a pyr is not enough. Taking care of a pyr does not substitute for their concerns being heard, for their inequities being addressed.

"If I say, there are opportunities I seek, the Seats would reply, 'But you have shelter and food.' I do not desire only shelter and food. I desire *voice*."

Uchitar curved a hand over his heart. Ador's hands were pressed against the table. Hin had drawn back into his seat, his lips still tight. Tum fidgeted, but did not interrupt.

Only when Volana rested back against her wings did Ador respond. "The Free Winds discuss these same ideas. While your concerns seem to focus on the lack of voice, ours rest more on the level of active control the Circles exert over us, the way they view themselves as caretakers of the pyrsi, rather than stewards of our trust. We do provide our voice, and they ignore it. They are a self-fulfilling device, you see. If there is not a problem to solve, they find a problem to solve. They never rescind their influence, only expand it. All in the name of *service*."

Ador's voice grew in intensity. "They serve us, the Circles say. Yet they praise each other, offer each other rewards and awards for this service. Imagine it. Servants, in a career of their choosing, paid for their work, rewarding each other, thanking each other with community resources—feeling themselves superior for it. And yet continuing to call it service, as if the term conveys humility."

Dime wasn't used to this harshness in Ador's speech, nor his frustration at matters of tone and philosophy rather than the more obvious debates over class and hemsa. She was starting to understand how hard he'd worked to protect her from this side of him while she'd worked in the Circles. How he'd set his own skepticism aside. The love of that—the unconditional love—stirred her, as much as it evoked her own guilt. A piece of her wished he had talked to her anyway, had those uncomfortable conversations.

Maybe, to move forward, pyrsi needed to be uncomfortable sometimes. Even among friends. Especially among friends.

"We have many factions in Sol's Reach," Ador continued. "The one that concerns me at this pass calls itself Sol's Pillars. They have . . . painted the Fo-ror as the enemy. As the threat to our security."

"We are no threat!" Volana nearly cried out.

"Then the Great War, was that invented?" Hin burst in. "Thousands of pyrsi didn't die, then? What do we say about that?"

While Ador had no charge over the younger pyr, he didn't hide his annoyance. "We're all on the same side here," he reminded. "Against the Violence."

"The Great War can't return." Hin's tone, while agitated, was sincere, concerned.

While not liking his tone or interruption, Dime saw his point: ignoring Sol's Pillars wasn't enough. Their rhetoric must be actively countered, or it could solidify in pyrsi's minds. "False words, stated often enough, can disguise themselves as truth," she'd warned her own children many times.

"We all agree." Ador swept his hand around, effectively pointing toward everyone in the room. "That's why we're here, right? To discuss what we can do."

"I'm interested in us working together," Uchitar said, unexpectedly. Luja smiled at him.

"I am also," Volana agreed. "We do not have these Sol's Pillars, but several groups have gathered in support of making contact with the Ja-lal. I went to one of the meetings once, to a group called the Risers."

"You didn't go again, though," Ador surmised.

"Correct. Their words hinted at reclaiming the Barrens—forgive me, Sol's Reach—reclaiming it in the name of peace. Their words were gentle and reasonable, the way they stated them. Yet, I was made uncomfortable, so I did not return. The Foundry, we focus on our own worries. We do not seek new ones." Volana looked up quickly. "Please, don't take that the Foundry would not reach out. I agree with you for that need. But it will be a shock to many."

"I understand," Ador said. "Solutions proposed with an inherent element of the Violence under the guise of peace are often more dangerous. Yet, we have the opposite now. I have never seen the Pillars so close to an open call." In his discomfort, Dime knew, he left off the rest of the sentence. *. . . to the Violence.*

As they continued to talk, Dime watched the reactions in the room. Tum was absorbed in every word, while Luja seemed to analyze each new idea. Uchitar had stood again, but shifted back and forth on both feet, with Agni sometimes winding around them.

Hin drew back, and though he intently followed each exchange, his skepticism was clear. Dayn's expression remained passive, except for the occasional glance to see how Dime was doing. Which was sweet.

In the center of all this, Ador and Volana leaned slightly in, reminding Dime, oddly, of a romantic painting, as engrossed as they were in the discussion.

Finally, Volana sighed. "I want to talk to you about so many things—unimportant things, as well as important. But I have a shift, and I must return for it. I am slower in flight these turns." She patted her midsection. "Let's speak again, soon. I wish I had more time." Rising from her seat, she smiled at each of them, in turn. "I truly do."

"Then it shall not be goodbye," Ador said rising and extending his arms, one palm up and one down, offering the intimate gesture known as the bridge, which signified connection, respect, an agreement between friends or partners. It was less friendly than a hug, but more serious. But did the Fo-ror have the same gesture? Dime wasn't sure.

Dime watched with awe as, whether by familiarity or instinct, Volana walked toward Ador and reached her arms, one under and one over, to link with his. Between Ador's short stature and Volana's extended middle, they were almost touching. The way Volana's worn ribbons waved against Ador's tailored suit moved Dime. More than just Ja-lal and Fo-ror met here, she realized.

She also realized that neither Volana nor Uchitar had showed any signs of valence. They must be aware how disorienting that could be on a first visit. Dime appreciated that sensitivity.

Deep in thought, she felt tired and overwhelmed all at once, and she lost a little track of the specifics as pyrsi greeted each other, exchanged information, and said goodbyes. "I hope we will meet again," she remembered Volana saying. Uchitar joked that they had a special meeting place, and Dime laughed, promising she would see them both again.

"Are you well?" Ador asked afterward, drawing near. The room felt less crowded, almost empty with the fairies gone.

"Feeling a little overwhelmed, I suppose."

"Then maybe this isn't the best time to talk. I have so much to work through, and I must return for a time. I'll come back here when I can, and if you're not here—you'll know where to find me. Most importantly, thank you for setting this up. It felt . . . meaningful."

"Thanks for not asking about my valence," she blurted in a whisper. "That means a lot."

Ador's expression grew serious. "Oh, Dime. This must be so much." He paused. "I was grateful they didn't raise it either. We need to keep valence out of the thoughts of Ja-lal as long as we can, until pyrsi can adjust." The look he gave her indicated he wasn't trying to poke at what had happened outside of Lodon, but Dime knew that couldn't happen again.

"I could tell tonight that I didn't need to explain that to Volana." He winced, as if thinking of something. "The Fo-ror may have mystical powers, but we are not powerless in Lodon. For now, any conversations must be easy. Controlled. And with pyrsi we trust."

"I'd put all my trust in you." Well, she would.

The worry washed from his face and he offered her a hug. "Sometimes I don't trust the world, Dime. Without Batu and without Dayn and you, I don't know if I could do it all."

"You could," Dime said.

"I'm glad I don't have to find out," he said. "Speaking of which, Volana was a good choice. If we can bring in pyrsi like her, we have a path of hope before us. I trust her. And Uchitar—he honors the ground she walks on, doesn't he?" Ador chuckled, not as if teasing, but as if touched.

She picked up that Ador had referenced walking, not flying, but yes, Uchitar's admiration for the generous fe'pyr was no secret. She didn't know anything about whether Uchitar had family or what his attractions were, but she didn't think he saw Volana in a romantic light. Whatever they had between them seemed much more . . . complex . . . than romance.

Hin joined them. He looked rattled; she knew that with his prejudices, this must have been a jarring meeting. It would be this way for most Ja-lal. Dime better get used to it. Hin better get used to it.

"Burgess Dime, it's been so nice to meet you."

Hopefully he'd have these positive interactions now to guide his thoughts. "It's been nice to meet you too, Hin. I'm sure I'll see you soon." She fanned her fingers, as Ador moved over to say goodbye to Dayn.

"Do you trust them?" Hin asked her, his voice low.

"Who? Volana and Uchitar? I do, yes." *I wouldn't have sent them to where my family was hiding if I didn't.*

"No, the fairies. All of them."

Dime worried at his words. But he was young, and he'd need time to process what he'd seen here. "I don't trust all of anyone." She tried to offer a light grin. "But that doesn't mean we shouldn't work together. Take the time you need. Think about it."

Hin smiled. "I suppose you're right. Well, thanks again. My best wishes to you." He fanned his fingers, then went to join Ador.

In her time in the Seats' complex, as well as here in the den, it bothered Dime immensely that she couldn't see outside. She'd never had a window in the IC towers either—one reason she'd appreciated her large home window—but at least back then, she could always get up and walk to one. In fact, that was a great idea.

She rose, walking up the curving stairs and opening the door to the outside. The skystones were bright tonight, and without many clouds, they cast an even glow across the plains. She nestled back into a hollow in the signal rocks, hidden from view in its shadows.

The door creaked again, and she had no doubt who'd come to join her. She smiled even before he arrived, and her smile did not fade as Dayn sat next to her, snuggling up against her side.

"I've missed you so much," she said. Dayn did not immediately answer. "How are you dealing with all of this?"

"I don't know. You've thrown a lot on me lately, you know. Sorry, that's not fair. I know it wasn't all you."

"The quitting was me."

"Not entirely." Dime was surprised by the response. "I know how they treated you there, how they treat anyone who questions how they operate. And, what, you're supposed to take it? For love of Sol?"

"Maybe I needed to. In order to make a difference."

"You'll make the most difference in the place you are most allowed to be you." Dayn's quick expression read almost like he'd said something offensive. His eyebrows flicked upward and he turned away. Dime normally could read Dayn's every expression, but this confused her a bit. This had all been confusing for her; of course it would be for Dayn as well.

"You know," she said, "when I went back to the IC after all of this, I thought I'd feel even more resentful. Instead, I remembered how much I liked the pyrsi there. Some are complacent, sure, but others work so hard. Maybe I wasn't the right one to improve things. But that doesn't mean someone can't."

"You couldn't stay there. I know that. I feel like I failed you, sometimes, not pushing you to leave sooner."

"I—" There were too many layers to it. Too much to say. So instead, she moved to something she'd been meaning to discuss, away from the kids. "Hey. Can we talk about the Boring Project?"

"Sure, it's my favorite subject." He tickled her knee.

"I think there's more going on with it. First, and I'd almost forgotten this, when I was escaping that first time, I saw machines boring far sur, probably close to here. Second, when I was in the IC records area, I saw fresh folders set out labeled with *Boring Project*, meaning they'd just printed new maps. And Beb wouldn't talk about them. Third . . . most importantly, when Rock and I were in the caves, there was frequent . . . shaking, and noises. Even from what seemed like a great distance, it gave us the sensation that the caves could collapse on top of us.

"What are the Circles doing?" she asked.

Dayn was silent a moment. "I feel like you'll be disappointed in me," he finally answered. She couldn't see his expression in the dark, but his voice stretched thin with concern. "It's not that I knew, exactly, but I think I should have. So many questions I had went unanswered. It was like I was part of the project, but also like they didn't want my involvement. I . . . I had wondered if it was because of you."

He squeezed her hand. "I mean, not . . . who you are. No one knew that, even me. I mean, just being in the IC. I resented that they were holding me back from information based on who my spouse was. And since they would never admit that, I couldn't confront them about it. I never stopped to think why there was such a secret in the first place. Everything you said . . . it fits."

It might not have just been Dime's position in the IC. She was known to ask questions, though clearly she hadn't asked enough. Yeah, they would have withheld information from him because of her. That ticked her off.

"So, are they trying to get to the diamonds?" she asked. "And why? To take them? Use them? Destroy them? Do they know what the diamonds can do? And either way," she continued, "the caves cover more area than I think they realize; the ground is less stable. They are putting the Fo-ror in danger."

"Harm." He paused to think about it. "Ja-lal are in danger, too, those living on that part of the plains."

Very few pyrsi lived out so far, and those who chose to, did so against the advisement of the Circles, who warned pyrsi to stay to the nor, for their safety. "Yes," Dime said, thinking through it, "but they also have a better chance to flee. The Fo-ror are at much more catastrophic risk if something goes wrong. Who knows how the water flows through the rocks? A collapse could devastate Pito."

"That's likely, if the city is close to the cliff. We've seen what the boring can do, up in a few of the mountains. No one lived there, but the damage we caused prompted a whole new set of guidelines." Dayn laughed without humor. "I thought we'd drawn the effort back."

Dime wished she'd been able to grab one of those new maps, but even without the specifics, it seemed they were in agreement on the potential consequences. Dime didn't want to say what she was thinking. As he often did, Dayn read her mind. Or, more likely, was thinking it too.

"The Circles know enough to know they're risking Fo-ror safety. They have to know. At best case, it's criminally negligent."

He left the worst case unspoken. But Dime knew. "Why, though?"

"Maybe . . . maybe if we get back to the city, I can find out more."

"You can't go back in." Not after his role in their leaving.

"Maybe not, but we still have contacts. Ador knows everyone. And your friends in the IC; someone would help."

Rock could do it. They'd never suspect her connection to Dime. A little wave of worry swept over her.

"Can I talk to you? About something else?"

"Of course." In the silence where she tried to figure out what she wanted to say, Dayn added, "We've had enough surprises; I think you can just tell me."

"Ok." She swallowed. "Rock and I were dating for a while, before I met you."

They both paused, with Dayn speaking first. "I figured that. When she found me in the city. She didn't say anything. Just . . . I figured."

Weird he'd picked up on that, she thought.

"It's fine," he continued. "Unless there's an issue?"

"No issue, it's just—" She wasn't sure what she was trying to say. "I still care about her."

He removed his hand from her knee with a pat. "Wouldn't it be strange if you didn't? Assuming it ended well? Or are you trying to tell me something?"

"There's no issue. I promise. I just . . . wasn't expecting it, and I didn't want you to think I was keeping anything from you."

He wrapped his arm around her. She had a feeling he was holding in his true reaction, but, well, she'd got that out and it wasn't like she needed to keep talking about it.

"I trust you," was all he said.

"I love you. Thanks . . . thanks for . . . listening. You're my best friend, you know?" She sighed. "When did everything get so difficult?"

"Not everything. Just a lot of things." Dayn rubbed her arm. "Before long, we need to spend some more time together."

There was no question what he meant. He felt like a magnet to her, even when talking about government and exes. She loved this ma'pyr. She did lean in a little, bringing her face close to his. "I agree." The idea that the kids could pop out at any moment kept the heat to a simmer, as it had a lot in the small den.

"Good." He laughed. "Good. If only we had a place to go. I mean, what are we, Aochs?"

So . . . that wasn't the way Dime thought of Aochs. They were youth, not— But that was absurd. An older Aoch was well into the age where some pyrsi were married and had a whole family. Pyrsi

Luja's age, she reminded herself, thinking back to her conversation with Ella.

"I've been trying to stop treating Luja like a ch'pyr." This was difficult to say. Dime wanted so much to be a good mother.

"It's tough. We're growing. As a family."

She was glad Tum was back, and she realized she hadn't even heard that part of the story. "Who brought her back? Tum, I mean."

"Juni did, all on her own."

Dime was trying to imagine Juni in the small den. She couldn't.

"She didn't really stay," he added. "She did, well, lick my face?"

That was an image that burst the tension. Dime laughed, immediately covering her mouth. She decided not to tell him that she'd seen Ella actually lick them back. He'd have to witness that one himself. "It's a sign of love. Trust me."

Dayn sighed.

Dime considered all he'd been through, and she welled with gratitude. "I love you so much. I'm so glad we're here, and I'm sorry about all of this. I'm so grateful for you. For all of us, but especially for you."

He ran his hand along her face.

"So what do we do?" she asked.

It was a serious question. She'd put it off until now, justifying that they were waiting for the fairies to arrive. The fairies had arrived. And left. Ever since her home had been invaded and Dime had run through the sewer pipes of Lodon, she'd had a clear next goal in mind. Something she needed to do before things could return to normal.

But what was normal now? Dime felt lost, confused, unsure of what was on her horizon. In a sense, that's what she'd wanted all along. Not just another shift in the towers. But, she'd thought she could start her music school, build a plan. She hadn't wanted to stay hidden away, with only a growing sense that she should and could help . . . and no clear way how.

"I don't know," was Dayn's first response. "We can't just stay here."

"The wallpaper," Dime agreed. "But, where?"

Dayn stretched his legs forward. She watched the silhouettes of his shoes against the landscape. "The problem is," he finally said, "no matter what you want, they aren't going to leave you alone. Fair or not. You're a disturbance to two governments who want to keep the calm and you're a lightning rod to anyone who doesn't."

Right. Like Sol's Pillars. And it didn't help that she'd already attacked them, either.

"It's more than just whether they'll leave me alone," she said. "You heard Ador and Volana—there's unrest on both sides of the cliff now. It's like when you feel the tiny rumble before an avalanche, you don't wait to get out of the way. The Ja-lal are losing their control based on the same fear they instilled in pyrsi to keep it. And the Fo-ror actually have kept pyrsi controlled, so much that they're beginning to reject it."

"You'd be so powerful to either side now," Dayn murmured. "It's so funny you don't care."

What? She *did* care; that was always the issue.

She reached for Dayn's hand again. "There's no side to take; that's my point. Harm it, I'm just not going to live scared; I've realized that. It would just be another version of what I did before. Maybe avalanche was the wrong analogy. It's like . . . the carts are moving on the same track. I'd rather guide them together than see them crash.

"But, then, I think of the risk. We have our children. They didn't ask for this. We don't even know who's the avalanche. Neimano's not my friend; I've got that. But the other Seats may now know I manipulated my way into the caves. I don't care—I'd do it again. But, what will they do? What will Ferala do?

"What happened in the city and how have Sol's Pillars used it? Have the Circles made me a criminal? Are they waiting to give me my hemsa? And what the harm are the Circles digging into the caves for? How am I supposed to figure any of it out, when now I'm on everyone's list? And all I ever did was quit my harmed-off *career!*"

"We'll work together," Dayn said, pulling closer. "We'll take care of the kids, and we'll do what we need to. We shouldn't have to live in fear. Or exile. We'll figure this out. Together. Besides, you have—"

They really hadn't discussed it. They needed to. "I can use valence. Turns out, lots of pyrsi can, but I have this crystal, and it's given me power that only I can use. I accept it now. It's part of who I am. Holding myself back is all I've ever done, and I'm not doing that anymore. I'm not."

"Here's what—" Dayn started to respond, but stopped. Dime turned to where he was looking. Only night spread before her.

"I saw lamps," he said. "Or a lamp, I don't know. It was way out there. The light flickered and then was gone."

Dime didn't have to say what they both knew. The nearby village was out of view of the den. So, either someone had wandered this way by coincidence or someone was out, looking for them. Or someone had found them.

"I dislike this wallpaper a lot," Dime said. Dayn gave her a squeeze.

It went unspoken but agreed: they needed to get out of there now.

"Hey, real quick?" Dayn pulled her in, and as their lips pressed together, her heart pounded as love flowed through her. More than desire, more than any valence, she felt love. For this pyr and their family and all the cycles ahead of them. If they could just get through this.

For all the effort it took to release him and stand, she barely heard his whispered words. "We'll figure it out," he said, offering her a hand up.

"I love you," she whispered. "Now, let's get out of here."

"Yes, Diamond," he answered, landing one more kiss, which she held—just a moment longer.

END OF PART 04

ABOUT THE AUTHOR

E.D.E. Bell was born in the year of the fire dragon during a
Cleveland blizzard. After a youth in the mitten, an MSE in
Electrical Engineering from the University of Michigan, three
wonderful children, and nearly two decades in Northern Virginia
and Southwest Ohio developing technical intelligence strategy, she
now applies her magic to the creation of genre-bending fantasy
fiction in Ferndale, Michigan, where she is proud to be part of
the Detroit arts community. A passionate vegan and enthusiastic
denier of gender rules, she feels strongly about issues related to
human equality and animal compassion. She revels in garlic. She
loves cats and trees. You can follow her adventures at edebell.com.

Continue Dime's story in . . .

Part 05: Voice

edebell.com/diamondsong

www.ingramcontent.com/pod-product-compliance
Lightning Source LLC
Chambersburg PA
CBHW032037180726
48284CB00008B/2628